UNFAIR

A NOVEL

TERRENCE BROTHERS

Library of Congress Cataloging-in-Publication Data is available upon request.

Paperback ISBN 978-1-7337303-6-5
Ebook ISBN 978-1-7337303-7-2

Cover design by Arcane Book Covers
Printed in USA

Books by Terrence Brothers available on Amazon

Unethical

Unfair

Unfair 2

Unethical 2

Unduly Sworn

Ungodly

CHAPTER 1

Only a month after moving to Vegas, Dr. James Goldwyn and his beautiful wife, Paige, stood naked on the balcony of their million dollar home appreciating the scenery of their immaculate backyard. Everything seemed normal and perfectly fine—they couldn't have asked for a setting that was more romantic. Just a few feet below from where they stood, lights illuminating from the large heated-swimming pool penetrated the darkness, displaying a body of crystal-blue water that couldn't have been more calm. Moisture from the pool, combined with the perfectly manicured garden that artfully lined the back wall, enabled a sweet welcoming scent produced by the roses to constantly linger beneath their noses.

"You know what's so amazing to me, sweetheart?" Paige said while moving closer.

"What's that?"

"We've been together for all these years and this euphoric feeling has never worn off."

"Neither has your beauty," Dr. Goldwyn replied.

As the night's air cooled their glistening skin, Paige smiled to herself while looking around as she pondered on the comment her husband had made, "I always enjoy making love to you out here, but I sometimes sense that someone is watching," she said as the moonlight accentuated her salacious curves. "What if our neighbors have a pair of binoculars and are getting their kicks out of watching us?"

"That's their prerogative," he said with a grin. "I mean, if we have the right to do whatever we want on our own property, I guess they have the right to watch from theirs."

"Mmmm," she said as she licked her lips. "If that's the case, then I'm pretty sure they enjoyed the show."

The lovebirds couldn't believe how quickly they had settled into their new environment. Living lavish was nothing new to the Goldwyn family. However, the Southern Highlands Community of Las Vegas was much more to their liking than the Beverly Hills mansion they moved from. The forty-three-year-old, interracial couple had needed a change of pace, so they decided to sell their California home and move their medical practice along with their eighteen-year-old identical twin daughters, Michelle and Melissa, out to Las Vegas where business was booming.

Before moving to Las Vegas, Dr. James Goldwyn had not claimed to be the only black man living in Beverly Hills, but he had been known to brag about being the youngest, most sought-after plastic surgeon that California had to offer. Considered by most to be egotistical, Dr. James Goldwyn had always been a man of confidence. Standing six feet three inches tall with an athletic build; he didn't depend solely on his good looks to get him by. He was also a great conversationalist, so instead of using tactics that other cosmetic surgeons had been known for using to solicit clients, his diplomatic style and flawless work compelled each of his clients to tell others about him.

When he was just a teen and one of the only few black kids attending Beverly Hills High School, James Goldwyn was dared by one of his classmates during his freshman year to approach the prettiest white girl in the school as she walked down the hallway toward her locker. He strolled up to her with the confidence of a lion and very calmly asked her to go out with him. To everyone's surprise, she said yes, and although no one knew it at the time, but their relationship would blossom and easily exceed anything that anyone could have ever imagined. She had seen the tall handsome football player around campus on several occasions, and had secretly developed a crush on him. The two remained an item throughout high school, even though many rumors began circulating around campus that he was frequently flirting with the cheerleaders of the school's football team. He vehemently denied the accusation, especially since it was said that he had been rejected by all of them. The former Paige Brinkmeyer quickly dismissed the rumors because she'd known that almost everyone attending the school had been jealous of she and James' relationship.

After graduation, the young attractive couple had been forced to endure a long-distance relationship while James went away to Harvard where he ultimately earned his degree in medicine. Ironically, they both came from families of which they were the only child, and neither of their parents approved of their interracial relationship. They were given an ultimatum to choose between one or the other. They chose each other, and right before James had been expected to return back to California from medical school, Paige rented a small apartment in North Hollywood where they lived for almost a year before they saved enough money and was finally able to afford to move to a bigger apartment. A few months later, not only had she learned that she was pregnant with twins, but James had managed to land an assistant's position at a well-known plastic surgeon's office in West Hollywood where he honed his skills as a plastic surgeon. In the years that followed, he managed to start his own medical practice and was well on his way to seeing success.

After performing countless procedures on many of Hollywood's A-list celebrities, Dr. James Goldwyn had not only made a name for himself, but he had become quite wealthy in only a short period of time.

At the ripe age of forty-three, Paige Goldwyn was still as beautiful and curvaceous as she was when she attended high school. When she gave birth to their precious twin daughters nearly two decades earlier, she experienced a mild case of post-partum depression—causing her to have low self-esteem, which resulted in her begging her husband to perform a few procedures on her. The most prevalent being breast implants, but also included liposuction, a tummy-tuck, and collagen shots to her already full lips. Standing five feet six inches tall with a voluptuous figure, she was possibly one of the most beautiful women to ever step foot in Las Vegas, Nevada. Most people would be shocked to learn; that underneath all of that beauty was a very inse-cure woman who was extremely fearful of being alone.

After holding each other for nearly an hour, the doctor and his wife grew tired of standing out on the balcony so they re-entered their home and shared a cocktail.

"So, what's our plan for tonight, sweetheart?" she asked in a seductive voice before sucking his finger inside her mouth.

"I don't think we really need a plan," he said before gasping—turned on by the sight of her pink-juicy tongue as it traveled up and down and in-between his fingers. "It's Friday night, the girls are out with their friends, and you and I are standing here alone naked. Should I say more?"

"It won't be necessary," she replied before kissing his lips.

As he lay on the small of his back propped up on his elbows, Dr. James Goldwyn closed his eyes and let his head fall back when his wife fell to her knees in between his legs and did the same to his dick as she'd done to his fingers. Both having very healthy libidos, once satisfied, he cracked a smile then laid flat on his back as she straddled his face so he could reciprocate the favor.

CHAPTER 2

Just before nine AM the following morning, the initials M&M inscribed in bold white letters appeared as bright as day beneath the front bumper of the black-on-black Range Rover, as it pulled into the driveway of their Pebble Street home. Parking directly behind their dad's H3 Hummer, Michelle and Melissa were full of excitement—which quickly dissipated when their mom and dad came storming from the house wearing facial expressions that was immediately alarming.

"Where the hell have you two been all night?" their dad growled as he approached the truck, noticing the two gentlemen who accompanied them.

"Dad, please don't embarrass us in front of our company," Michelle pleaded as the two gentlemen excited the backseat. "Meagan and Alix decided to go home early so we went to a party with Rashad and Marcus. We were meaning to call but I guess we sort of lost track of time."

"Girls, this kind of behavior is totally unacceptable. Your mother and I have been worried to death," he said while making an attempt to control his anger. "Not only did you not bother calling us, but I couldn't get in touch with

either of you. Before you left here last night, you specifically said that you were going to be out with Meagan and Alix. I called Meagan a few hours ago and she had no clue where you girls were at," he said with his lips quivering. "She's been home since ten-something last night—here it is, almost nine AM and you show up at my door like nothing is wrong."

"Dad, we're sorry," Melissa interrupted.

"You should be sorry," he shot back. "We've only been out here for a month and you're already running around town with guys twice your age. You know I didn't raise you two to be like this."

"Hold on, man! These are grown women you're talking to," the older of the two men blurted out. "I don't know who you think you are or who you think you're talking to, but I'm sure you can see that it ain't no fuckin' kids out here, right?"

"Young man, these are my daughters and I'm their dad, so don't you dare bring your ass on my property and try to tell me how to talk to mine!" Dr. Goldwyn said as he stepped closer. "Who might you be anyway, and how old are you?"

"I'm Marcus, and I'm twenty-five," the young man retorted, his ego not allowing him to back down.

Back when he was an active gang member, Marcus who was better known as M-80, had earned a reputation for shooting people in the act of committing home-invasion style robberies, but he's changed his life tremendously since then. He was fully aware that he still needed to work on correcting his attitude problem, but he found the process to be extremely difficult,

especially in situations like these when he felt like he was being challenged. He stood there dressed in a bright-orange outfit, the same color as a prison jumpsuit, and a pair of navy blue K-Swiss sneakers with a matching Houston Astros baseball cap—colors that were widely known to be worn and associated with an infamous street gang known as the Hoover Crips. His temperature slowly continued to rise as he stared at Dr. Goldwyn, who continued speaking.

"Marcus, my babies are only eighteen years old and you're much too old to be hanging with them," he said while towering over the young man. "This is not how I raised my daughters. I raised them better than this, and I definitely didn't expect them to be hanging around guys who look like you. Look at you, showing up at my house wearing these baggy ass pants with braids in your head. Intelligent people don't dress like that. What in the world could you possibly do for my daughters, and what the hell could they possibly see in either of you?"

"Dad, let me take them home," Michelle demanded as she stepped in front of Marcus and began lightly pushing him backwards toward the truck. "I would have never brought them over here if I knew you were gonna act like this."

"Yeah, take me home," Marcus told her. "If he wasn't your pops, I would pop a cap in his punk-ass for disrespecting me. I don't play that shit and that fool better be lucky he's getting a pass. Motherfuckers usually don't get away with shit like that, especially when dealing with a motherfucker like me," he stated arrogantly.

"Shut up, Marcus and get in the truck!" Michelle yelled as she hurried toward the driver's side then climbed behind the steering wheel.

Once the twins and their friends were inside the truck, both Mr. and Mrs. Goldwyn were visibly shaken as they headed up the walkway toward their home, more desperate than ever to feel a sense of security. Dr. Goldwyn had worked extremely hard to provide for he and his family, and although he and his wife had long suspected the girls of being sexually active, these were exactly the kind of guys that he prayed his daughters wouldn't be attracted to. He felt they deserved the best of everything, and he planned to do everything in his power to make them want for themselves what he wanted for them.

Inside the Range Rover, Rashad and Melissa remained quiet while Michelle and Marcus continued arguing. The twins had met these gentlemen two weeks prior on the Las Vegas Strip while browsing around the Forum Shops at the Caesars Palace Hotel. And, just like then, Melissa and Rashad remained quiet while Michelle and Marcus were the loquacious ones. When it came to comparison, the twins' distinctive personalities were the only thing that allowed others to tell them apart. Sharing the same cute faces, the same five foot curvy physiques, and the same short hairstyle as their mothers', their conflicting personas were the only thing that made them different. Taking after her father, Michelle Goldwyn was known for being outspoken. Her confidence and assertiveness had easily earned her the title of being the evil twin. Unlike Melissa, who possessed a quiet timid demeanor, a lot similar to her mother's.

Nearly twenty minutes after beginning their journey, the black Range

Rover came to a complete stop in front of a three-story apartment complex on the corner of 28th Street and Cedar Avenue. Without bothering to turn around, Michelle paused for a moment and took a deep breath before switching off the truck's ignition and reluctantly peered up at the rear-view mirror, "Marcus, I don't appreciate the way you disrespected my dad back there. Because of the comments you made and your inability to keep your mouth shut, I think it'll be best for us if we discontinue our relationship."

"That's how you feel, huh?" he responded in a low voice, showing that he didn't care one way or another.

"That's how I feel," she said as she restarted the truck's engine.

As both men slowly opened their doors to emerge from the vehicle, Rashad slightly squeezed Melissa's shoulder before rubbing it gently and saying good-bye, "This doesn't end our friendship, does it?"

"Of course not. I'll call you later," she said with a look of innocence, toying with his hand before he eased it from her grip then closed the door.

Once the truck made a complete u-turn, Michelle pressed heavily on the accelerator then sped up 28th Street in the same direction that they'd traveled from, "That's a shame," she said while nodding her head. "Rashad is only twenty-one and acts more like Marcus's older brother than his younger one."

"He's twenty, but he will be twenty-one in a couple of weeks," Melissa said.

"I think the two of you would make a nice couple."

"You think so?" she asked, not really expecting to get an answer.

"Yeah. Not only is he cute, but he seems to have a lot of respect for you. More importantly, he knows how to keep his mouth shut, and that's a lot more than I can say for his older brother."

"I'll think about it," Melissa replied. "Right now I just need to get home and get some sleep."

"I hear you on that, girl," Michelle said.

Only two weeks after they moved to Vegas, the twins was hanging out in the waiting room of their dad's office when they struck up a conversation with one of his potential clients. They'd seen the tall beautiful redhead on several occasions, and each time they'd seen her, she had done nothing but smile and would always have some kind of camera taking pictures. She introduced herself as Meagan Duboise, and the twenty-three-year old had been visiting Dr. Goldwyn's office nearly every day because she was strongly considering getting breast implants. Although her dream was to someday become a professional photographer, she was currently working as a full-time receptionist at her best friend Alix's massage parlor. The A-One massage parlor had just opened it doors two months prior when Meagan, who was only interested in seeing her wages increase, offered the twins some buy-one-get-one-free massage coupons—hoping to persuade them both into becoming new clients. When they went over the following day, the twins found themselves to be quite impressed when they were formally introduced to the parlor's owner. Alix Onefeather was a twenty-four-year-old Native American beauty who had long silky black hair reaching the center of her back. In less than an hour of conversation, she was equally impressed with the twins, so she hired them both as her new assistants. A move she felt completely comfortable with, knowing that just by having identical twins working for her, could be a great way to further promote her new business.

Taking an entire week to personally train the twins, Alix was so excited about her business' future—she felt more than certain she'd made a sound investment. Trying to come across as being more professional than she actually was, she gave the twins intricate details about how she expected her business to run, percentages they would be expected to pay, and also informed them that they would be fully responsible for establishing their own clientele, and would also have to purchase their own supplies—a feat they soon proved was no problem for them.

Usually the twins had to be at work on Saturday mornings, but since Alix was having the parlor's interior repainted a more vibrant color, she gave them the entire weekend off, hoping to prevent them all from subjecting themselves to fumes that was possibly harmful.

As soon as Michelle turned on Pebble Street, she brought the Range Rover to a screeching halt to avoid crashing into the vehicle that swerved in front of her.

"Watch where you're going, bitch!" the driver shouted as if he wasn't at fault.

"Fuck you!" she yelled back.

With a look that could have only meant disgust, Michelle shot a quick glance in Melissa's direction as she stepped on the gas—cussing under her breath. The driver who had blatantly called her a bitch was their next door neighbor, Charlie Walker. Everyone called him Bull—a name perfectly suiting for his stockiness and bull-headed demeanor, she thought. Because Bull had always been rude to her, Michelle felt nothing but hatred towards the man and assumed that his only reason for disliking her was the fact that she wouldn't have sex with him. However, both she and Melissa had nothing but good things to say about his roommate, Anthony Bagly. Everyone referred to him as Amp, and Michelle learned through him that he and Bull co-owned an escort service. Besides Bull proving that he was rude and self-centered, he and Amp were pretty good neighbors who kept to themselves for the most part. Michelle had no idea why, but she despised the fact that the two men had beautiful women constantly running in and out of their home, that she was more than certain they were having their way with.

She and Melissa were extremely exhausted when they entered the house that possessed all of the markings of a privileged family. After climbing the stairs and entering their parent's bedroom, they apologized for Marcus's rude behavior—gave each of their parents a kiss on the cheek, and were soon in their bedrooms sound asleep.

CHAPTER 3

Emergency Dispatcher Charlene Moon had just begun her shift when she felt herself craving a hot cup of coffee. It was just before daybreak Monday morning, and since she was filling in for a co-worker who had called in sick, her place of employment was the last place she wanted to be on what was supposed to be the only off day she'd had in weeks. Reminding herself of how serious her job was, she pushed whatever selfish feelings she had aside, and adjusted her headset to take a call, "911, what's your emergency?"

"Please send someone to my address, I think my husband is dead!" a woman said in a frantic voice.

"Calm down ma'am. Who am I speaking with?"

"My name is Paige Goldwyn and my husband's been shot. Oh my god, please hurry up and send somebody!"

"Calm down, Paige. Someone will be there shortly," the dispatcher said while typing quickly. "Paige, do you know who shot your husband?"

"No!" she said dryly. "I woke up and we were both lying in bed covered in blood."

"Did you hear any gunshots?"

"I didn't hear anything, I was asleep. Please send somebody, is anyone coming?"

"Stay calm, ma'am. The police have already been notified," the dispatcher said before the line went dead.

Moments later, Paige Goldwyn could not stop herself from trembling when she heard the patrol cars pulling up. As soon as she heard the sirens and saw red and blue lights flashing outside of her living room window, still extremely shaken, she immediately stood up from where she was sitting on the flight of stairs and greeted the police officers as they reached the front door.

"Are you Mrs. Goldwyn?" a young officer asked.

"Yes, I am," she said while sobbing, offering no other words as she stood in shock.

"Did you call 911 to report a shooting?" he asked while peering inside.

"Yes," she mumbled. "My husband's been shot. He's right upstairs."

It didn't take long for the two uniformed officers to find Dr. Goldwyn's lifeless body lying naked in the center of the bed in a large puddle of his own blood. He had been shot once in the head, and if it weren't for the gaping hole on the left side of his temple, and the large amount of splattered brain, bone, and blood that matted his pillow, he could have easily been mistaken for being asleep.

Michelle and Melissa, who was still wearing their pajamas, remained close to each other as they were ushered down the stairs by a uniformed officer who had just denied them access to their parents bedroom, "Mom, what's going on, what's happening?" Melissa asked in a scared voice.

Instead of answering immediately, Paige waited until her daughters reached the bottom of the staircase before she pulled them aside and held them tightly, "Your dad's been hurt, honey."

"Hurt how, what happened to him?" Michelle asked as more emergency personnel entered the house.

"Your dad's been shot, I think he's probably dead," she replied as tears fell from her eyes.

As they stood there sobbing and consoling each other, the young uniformed officer who had been one of the first to arrive on the scene, quickly ran down the stairs and pulled Paige aside before he glanced over his shoulder to make sure no one could hear him, "Mrs. Goldwyn, did you shoot your husband?"

"Why would you ask me something like that?" she looked surprised, not really wanting to show how offended she was. "No, I did not shoot my husband."

"Well, how do you explain not seeing anybody or hearing anything?" the officer asked. "Weren't you in bed lying next to him?"

"Yes I was, but I was asleep," said Paige.

"What about the patio door, how did that get opened?"

"I have no idea. That's the way it was when I woke up and found my husband like that," she said as more tears streamed down her face. "I didn't touch anything. All I did was call the police and change my nightgown be-cause it was covered in blood."

"That leads to my next question, Mrs. Goldwyn," he said as he eyed her closely. "I saw the bloody nightgown lying on the bedroom floor. How often did you go to bed wearing a nightgown when your husband was in bed completely naked? Are you menstruating or something?"

"Don't you think that's kind of personal?" she asked, as if she couldn't believe he'd asked the question. "No, I'm not on my cycle and I don't think it's anyone's business what my husband and I do in the privacy of our bed-room."

"Well, Mrs. Goldwyn, being that it was only you and your husband occupying that bedroom, you leave us no other choice but to suspect that you're responsible for the man's death. At this time, I would like to inform you of your rights. You have the right to remain silent, anything you say can and will be used against you in a court of law …"

"This is unfair, Officer Graham," she said as she noticed his name tag. "I had absolutely nothing to do with my husband's death."

"I advise you to stop talking, Mrs. Goldwyn. You'll have plenty of opportunities to do that when you see a judge," he explained as he grabbed her arm, cuffing her wrists behind her back.

This can't be happening, Paige told herself. It all felt like a horrible nightmare. Not only had she lost her soulmate, but the fact that her daughters had to watch her be arrested for a crime that she hadn't committed was dev-astating to her, and she fought back tears as they cried in agony. It seemed as if all were lost and their worlds were beginning to crumble around them.

"Why is she being arrested, she didn't do anything," Melissa yelled.

"Girls, I'm sorry, but your mom is being placed under arrest for your father's murder," Officer Graham explained. "You two should probably grab some clothes. This house is officially a crime scene and we'll be asking you to leave until we wrap up our investigation."

"How long will that take?" Michelle asked, still in disbelief about what was happening.

"My guess is about four or five hours," the officer replied.

"Where are you taking her and when can we see her?" Melissa chimed in.

"She'll be going downtown to the Clark County Detention Center. Once we book her in, you can call down there and they'll be able to tell you when she'll be allowed to have visitors."

"Girls, don't ever forget how much mommy loves you," Paige interjected. "I haven't done anything wrong, so stay strong for me and I'll be home soon."

"You'll have to explain that to the judge, ma'am," the officer said as he guided her toward the front door.

Once they exited the large house and walked down the walkway, Paige Goldwyn slowly looked around to see if any of her neighbors were looking to see what was happening. In doing so, she made eye contact with a plainclothes police officer as he stepped outside of his unmarked cruiser. Appearing to be in his late forties to early fifties, the tall, clean-shaven handsome detective found himself in awe by the woman's beauty, but quickly averted his eyes and headed towards the house. A short time later, both Michelle and Melissa were seen making their exit as officers blocked off the entrance with yellow crime-scene tape.

Two hours after being processed and booked into the Clark County Detention Center, Paige Goldwyn was sitting inside of a cold holding cell when an officer came to inform her that she had a visit. Excited to see her daughters' beautiful faces, her anticipation continued to grow, but after being escorted to an interview room, she was pleasantly surprised to see the handsome detective she'd seen at her home.

"Hello, Mrs. Goldwyn, please have a seat," he said as he struggled to avoid making eye contact. "My name is Detective Frank Bruno, and I'll be in charge of this investigation."

"Detective Bruno, huh?" she said while thinking out loud. "It kind of has an Italian ring to it, but you don't really look Italian to me."

"Offending me is probably not the best way to start, Mrs. Goldwyn. Not only was I born in Sicily, but both of my parents were full-blooded Italians as well. Unfortunately, they both passed away a few years back."

"Oh, I'm sorry to hear that," she said—instantly regretting her previous remark. "I apologize if I offended you; I hope you can find it in your heart to forgive me."

"Don't worry about it," he said politely, noticing that she was more beautiful up close than he'd previously thought. "How are you holding up?"

"I'm holdin'."

"Good," he said before placing his notepad in front of him. "I have a few questions I need to ask you."

"Shoot."

"What kind of relationship did you have with your husband?"

"My husband and I had a great relationship," she said as her voice saddened. "It seems so unreal to me, and I still can't believe that he's actually gone."

"Well, he's definitely gone that's why I'm here," he stated coldly, not bothering to conceal his ruthlessness.

Frank Bruno was known for being a hard-nosed detective. He had been a Las Vegas cop for over thirty years—more than twenty of those years in the homicide department. In his repertoire, he was a highly-decorated officer—known for countless acts of bravery, and though he did sometimes use tactics that was sometimes questionable, he was highly respected within the community and was simply described as being firm but fair, "Mrs. Goldwyn, do you know what really bothers me?"

"What's that, detective?"

"When I first laid eyes on you and saw how beautiful you were, I could not believe it when I entered that gorgeous house and saw a black guy lying across the bed."

Clearly confused, Paige thought for a moment before replying, "I don't really understand your point, detective, but the answer is no if you're asking me if I killed my husband."

"To be perfectly honest with you, I wouldn't give a shit if you did,

Mrs. Goldwyn," he stated bluntly, then had the audacity to wink at her. "I was just going to say that I personally don't think he deserve a woman like you. What was he, some kind of doctor or something, right?"

Feeling a bit uneasy about the detective's remarks, she sensed that he was intentionally being disrespectful and she wasn't in any mood to play games, "A plastic surgeon, and a very good one I might add."

"Is that who did your fine work?"

"It is, but what does that have to do with anything?"

"It could become relevant later on. Anything is possible with these sorts of cases," he said while scratching his head. "I gotta admit though, he definitely did a great job."

"When can I go home, Detective Bruno, or am I going to need a lawyer for that?"

"Well, I'm sure you will need a lawyer eventually, but you won't need one while you're talking to me," he said as he looked at his notes. "As far as you getting out, you'll first have to appear before a judge and see if he'll either set you a bail or release you on your own recognizance. Right now, you have no bail because you're being charged with a very serious offense."

"When will I see a judge?" she asked with tears in her eyes.

"I can't say for certain, but I'm sure it'll probably be sometime this week," he said before crossing out something he'd previously written. "Mrs. Goldwyn, you said that you and your husband had a great relationship, right?"

"Correct."

"Besides the house, I saw some pretty expensive vehicles parked on the property. Do you work for a living, or was your husband the sole provider?"

"I don't know what you're implying, detective, but I worked my ass off at my husband's practice," she said, giving off a tinge of anger that didn't go unnoticed.

"Where's that, and what was your position?"

"I was my husband's receptionist, and the practice is located on Cactus and Southern Highlands Parkway."

"I'm vaguely familiar with that area," he said while jotting it down. "And the two of you have never had any problems?"

"Of course we have. We were married for eighteen years and we both could be very ambivalent at times," she answered honestly. "We had our ups and downs just like anyone else, but we've always found a way to work things out."

"Except for this time?" he asked, as if he suspected her of withholding something.

"What do you mean except this time? I did not kill my husband, detective. If I'm not mistaken, I believe that I've already told you that."

"Mrs. Goldwyn, do you know of anyone who might have wanted your husband dead? An ex-lover, an ex-business partner. Is there anyone you can think of who might have wanted to see him dead?"

"I can't think of anyone," she replied in a low voice. "Since we moved out here, the only people he dealt with were his clients, which consisted mainly of strippers and showgirls. Unless someone came from California and did this to him," she thought to herself before a thought suddenly occurred to her. "Oh, wait a minute. He did have an argument with this guy the other day."

"Do you know his name?" he asked with interest.

"He mentioned it but I can't recall it—he's one of the guys that my daughters brought to the house," she said, looking directly at him. "During the argument, the guy threatened to shoot my husband, saying he had been disrespectful or something."

"What does this guy look like?"

"He's a black gang-banger type, who looked to be somewhere in his mid-twenties."

"Did anyone else witness this argument, and can anyone else corroborate your story?"

"Everyone heard it," she said in a high-pitched voice. "It happened in the driveway of my home two days ago. My daughters could tell you more about it if you talk to them. They came home with two guys that day and I'm sure they can tell you who they both were."

"And this was two days ago?" he asked suspiciously.

"Yes, Saturday morning," she answered promptly.

"And he's a friend of your daughters?"

"I'm not sure whose friend he is, but he's one of the two guys they brought home that day."

"Are your daughters employed?" he inquired.

"Yes, they're both masseuses at the A-One massage parlor next door to the practice."

Once he wrote down all of the information she provided him with, Detective Bruno wiped the sweat from his forehead before scooting his chair back, preparing to leave, "Okay, Mrs. Goldwyn, that's all the help I'll need for now. I appreciate your cooperation and I will be checking the details of the statement you just gave me. If I have any more questions, I'll be sure to come down and speak with you. Until then, stay safe and take care of yourself," he said as he stood up.

A few moments after the interview ended, Detective Frank Bruno strolled out of the Clark County Detention Center, eager to look into the story he had just received. Meanwhile, after being escorted back to a holding cell, Paige Goldwyn could no longer control her emotions as tears rushed from her eye ducts like levees had broken. Feeling completely lonely and empty inside, she knew with no doubt in her mind that a piece of herself had also died when her husband had taken his last breath.

CHAPTER 4

"Oooh, bitch you got some good pussy!" Bull said as he thrust himself deeper inside of her. "You know I like hittin' this ass from the back."

"I know, daddy. Get this pussy," Veronica screamed while spreading her ass cheeks, then bending over farther so he could go even deeper. "It feels so good, daddy. I want you to fuck me until you can't fuck no more."

Standing five six weighing two hundred and fifty-five pounds, Bull's massive body was drenched in sweat as he closed his eyes then released his sperm. He and Veronica had spent the last several hours relishing in sex about forty-five minutes after taking ecstasy. She was his favorite, and was one of six girls who worked for him and Amp's escort service, that he sexed on occasion when he was high on X. Veronica's body had more curves than a coca-cola bottle with a smooth dark complexion resembling milk chocolate. Not only was Veronica very attractive, but Bull appreciated the fact that it turned her on tremendously when he bad-mouthed her.

As he lay naked on the black leather sofa—exhausted from overexerting himself, Bull used a damp green cloth to wipe the sweat from his forehead as Veronica ran her long wet tongue around his sensitive nipple, "That's enough, bitch!" he snapped at her.

"What's wrong daddy, you can't go no more?" she asked, laughing.

"Hell nah, you got my nuts empty as a motherfucker. Give me a minute and let me catch my breath," he said as he laid back, before covering his face with the damp cloth.

"Ah, poor baby, did I drain you?" Veronica teased, knowing how much he hated it when she taunted him. "That's the same thing that I do to all my tricks. I haven't found anyone yet who knew how to keep up with me."

"Trick?" Bull rapidly uttered. "Talkin' like that will get you fucked off. You must wanna get found the way they found that doctor next door? You know somebody went in there and popped his ass, right?"

"Yeah, I heard about it. Amp told me about it the day it happened, then I turned around and saw that shit on the news. That's fucked up."

"It's gon' really be fucked up if you call me another trick 'cause they gon' fuck around and find you the same way," Bull said as he playfully tapped her on the forehead.

An hour later, Bull was still feeling the effects of the powerful drug when he woke up naked on the living room couch, "Veronica," he said in a voice that was barely audible, his hands feeling around lazily in the dark for her. There was no answer. It was completely silent, maybe she got up and went to the bathroom, he wondered? A few minutes went by but there was still no sound. There wasn't a peep in the entire house, the only sound that he could hear was himself breathing. Realizing Veronica was gone, Bull suddenly leapt to his feet then stealthily made his way across the living room floor—for no specific reason, he found himself nervous. He wasn't the type to panic or get paranoid, but he wanted to be certain that the front door was locked. It was. Veronica had made sure of it before she left the residence twenty minutes earlier. While Bull was asleep on the living room couch, she had received an urgent text message from Amp on her cell phone, telling her that it was very important that she go meet with a gentleman at the Palazzo Hotel.

Two weeks later, Michelle and Melissa were still grieving the death of their father who had just been buried the week before. Even though their mom remained in jail, they found themselves feeling slightly better after the funeral because several of their dad's closest friends and old clients had traveled from California to pay their last respects. Although they hadn't been to work in nearly a week, the twins' bond with Meagan and Alix continued to grow because they started spending a lot more time together. The first week after their dad was killed, Michelle and Melissa could not decide on whether or not they should move or stay at home and it was Meagan and Alix who had comforted them. And though their Pebble Street house didn't feel like home anymore, instead of opting to live with Meagan or Alix, their mom talked them into staying at home—she made them believe it's what their dad would have wanted. Melissa, who had usually been the conservative twin, had become more promiscuous and did a lot more drinking as she struggled to cope with her father's death. Each time she and her sister went to the jail to visit their mother, Melissa would always burst into tears because it saddened her deeply to see her mom confined. Truly believing in their mother's innocence, it made things twice as hard to have to visit with her over a TV monitor instead of up close and personal where they could hug each other.

When Paige attended her arraignment, she pled not guilty to the charge of first- degree murder and the judge who had been appointed to preside over the case had denied her request to set a bail. She hoped to be out with her daughters until the trial began but, instead, a preliminary hearing date was set, and since she desperately wanted to prove her innocence, Paige took the advice of her fellow inmates and hired, who was considered to be one of Las Vegas's best defense attorneys to represent her, because she knew that she would need competent representation. Four days before her scheduled arraignment, she received a visit from Detective Bruno, informing her that he had looked into the allegations made at their initial meeting, and even though other witnesses agreed that an argument between Marcus and Dr. Goldwyn had in fact taken place, Marcus provided an alibi for the morning of Dr. Goldwyn's death, and after looking into it—it checked out. Armed with this information, being that she was the only suspect in custody, Paige knew that she would be the one tried for her husband's murder and that it would take a good lawyer to prove her innocence. Known to be one of the best lawyers that money could buy, Defense Attorney Donald Brown had earned a reputation for coming up with some of the most craftiest strategies when it came down to defending his clients. However, this case was different. Being a black man himself, he had never faced a challenge of defending a white client who was being accused of killing a black person. Having a perfect trial record of sixty-two wins and zero losses; he could have possibly just taken a case that could prove to be the most challenging of his entire career. With absolutely no strategy in mind, after visiting with his client at the Clark County Detention Center, he wondered for the first time in his seventeen years of practicing law, if he had made a mistake by taking the case?

CHAPTER 5

Rashad Myers' anticipation continued to escalate as he sat on the passenger's side of his brother's car, "I really appreciate this ride, man," he chuckled as they waited for the light to turn green. "I know you and your girl had plans for tonight but I'm glad you were able to do me this favor."

"Man, don't worry about it," Marcus replied. "It's your birthday, and I can definitely understand you wanting to spend time with your girl—I'm sure I would want to do the same thing. Andrea and I really didn't have anything planned. She probably just wanted me to chill with her so we could smoke a few blunts until it came time for me to get deep in that ass. You know how we operate."

Almost ten years his senior, Andrea Shaw was a tall light-skinned woman with long black hair and extraordinary beauty who had two beautiful daughters from previous relationships. She grew up a military brat and was awfully close to her dad before he died. She and Marcus had been together for six months, and not only had they become incredibly close, but he'd fallen in love with her two daughters and he treated them both as if they were his own since neither of their biological fathers were in the picture.

Pressing heavily on the gas of his Honda Accord, Marcus Myers sat with a look of arrogance spread across his face before turning to Rashad, who appeared to be in deep thought, "Tell me this though," he said before pausing. "With all the time that you've been spending with Melissa, has she allowed you to tap that ass yet?"

"Nah man, not yet," Rashad replied. "But that's exactly what I'm hoping to do tonight," he continued, proudly holding up a condom that he removed from his pocket. "I'm always prepared just in case."

"That's right, lil' bro. Regardless of how good these females look, you can never be too safe when dealing with them. Make sure you strap up every time," said Marcus, glad to see that his younger brother wasn't a crashdummy. "Man, are you saying that when she took you to the movies the other night, the girl didn't give you no kind of play?"

"Uh-uh. All I got was a kiss that night. That's as far as she ever allows me to go, so I'm assuming she's waiting until the time is right?"

"Your game must not be strong enough," Marcus teased. "If I hadn't pissed Michelle off, I know I'd be done hit that ass by now," he said as he switched lanes. "I'll tell you what, though. Today is your birthday and there will never be a better time than this."

"That's what I'm saying," Rashad agreed, playfully raising his hand to pop his collar.

"If you don't get that pussy tonight, I think you might as well hang it up."

"I think tonight might turn out to be the night, I heard it in her voice when she called this morning. When she told me to come to her job tonight, she said to catch a cab if I had to. Why else would she tell me that if she didn't have plans of doing anything?"

"I can't answer that, lil' bro, but I guess we'll know in a couple of minutes."

The atmosphere was pleasant inside of the massage parlor, unlike any other business they had ever entered. Everything was so immaculate, and the layout of the place was breathtaking. Instantly impressed by the parlor's professional décor, Marcus suddenly seemed to feel a bit uneasy—he sensed that the patrons who sat inside the lobby were eerily staring at them out the corner of their eyes. Rashad was feeling so good about his prospects for the evening, that he hadn't even noticed that they were being watched. He asked his brother to wait for him by a magazine rack before heading off quickly towards the receptionist's desk.

"Oh, hi Rashad," Meagan said cheerfully, displaying a set of perfect white teeth as she smiled at him. "Give me a minute and I'll let Melissa know that you're here to see her."

"Thanks, Meagan," he replied before heading back toward where Marcus was sitting.

"Damn, who is that amazon?" Marcus whispered.

"Who?"

"That tall ass redhead you just finished talking to."

"Oh, that's Meagan, she's cool," Rashad replied.

"I bet she's a freak, too," Marcus added. "I definitely wouldn't mind gettin' with that."

A few moments after leaving her desk, Meagan Duboise reappeared from the dimly-lit hallway looking just as stunning as she had when she'd left. Wearing a tight black dress that barely covered her thighs, several customers who sat in the lobby were getting their kicks out of watching her, "She'll be out in a minute, Rashad," she said while hurrying toward her desk to answer the phone.

"Thank you," Rashad replied before noticing how Marcus was staring at her. "Man, don't you already have a girl?"

Realizing he was caught, Marcus grinned at his younger brother as he tried his best to play it off, "I do, but she's not like that. Man, do you see how fine that girl is? Tall, thick and pretty, just the way I like 'em. Go ahead and hook that up for me."

"Hook what up?" Rashad asked, not really in the mood for sarcasm. "Man, that girl is not thinking about you. She's as square as they come and all she really likes doing is taking pictures."

"If that's the case, I got something that she can take a picture of," Marcus said as they both laughed.

Enjoying each other's company, Rashad and Marcus continued laughing, until Melissa—whose smile quickly faded away when she entered the lobby and spotted Marcus.

"What is he doing here?" she asked in a voice that spelled disaster when Rashad climbed to his feet and walked over to greet her. "I told you to catch a cab if you had to."

"Baby, I didn't have money to catch a cab, so I asked my brother to drop me off," he explained.

Melissa stood in anger as she peeked over Rashad's shoulder, trying to keep Marcus from hearing their conversation, "Rashad, if he had dropped you off, this discussion we're having would be non-existent. You know my sister is gonna have a fit if she comes out here and sees him here."

"Yeah, you're right. Give me a second and let me talk to him."

Reluctantly, Rashad spun around and approached Marcus, who seemed to already sense that something was wrong, "What's up, man?" he asked.

"Nothing really, she just doesn't want Michelle to come out here and see you here," said Rashad.

Marcus covered his face with his hands and shook his head, upset but fought hard to contain himself, "Man, I don't know why that girl think I killed her pops. I had nothing at all to do with that, and I don't appreciate them sending that detective to the house to talk to us like that," he said loud enough for Melissa to hear.

"Bro, calm down before you cause a scene in here," Rashad said while looking around. "We both know what's up man, but there's nothing you can do until this court shit is over with. As far as that detective goes—that man interviewed everybody and he explained that to us when he talked to us."

"Yeah, I know, but he also said that they were the ones who sent him to us."

"Man, let's leave this alone," Rashad retorted. "If you hadn't said the shit you said that day we wouldn't be going through none of this bullshit."

"Alright, man. Let me go ahead and get out of here before Michelle comes out and starts running her mouth," he said as he changed the subject and began backing up slowly towards the front entrance. "Enjoy your birthday, lil' bro. Don't forget what we talked about and don't hesitate to call if you need a ride."

"Alright, man," Rashad nodded.

Feeling like his dream was about to become reality, Rashad readily allowed his eyes to close after Melissa approached him smiling, wearing a pair of pink pants that fit so snugly that she could have coined the term camel-toe. She stood with both hands clasp to her hips before extending her arms then wrapping them around him, "Happy birthday, baby."

"Thank you," he replied as Melissa laid her head gently against his chest. "So, why was it so important for me to come out here?"

"Because, I wanted to see my man on his birthday," she said seductively, as she took a step backwards and posed for him. "Plus, I got something special that I want to do for you."

"Is that right?" he anxiously replied.

"That's right. You know what I need you to do for me?" she asked flirtatiously.

Not wanting to appear to be overexcited, Rashad paused for a moment to lick his lips, then stared Melissa up and down before replying, "What's that, baby?"

"I need you to strip down naked and wrap yourself in a towel for me," she said while pulling him toward the nearby hallway. "Do you think you'll be able to handle that?"

"Of course I can," he answered quickly.

Once they entered a back room, Melissa guided Rashad straight to the massage table before she turned to him and began speaking, "I'll be right back, but I need you to lay face down for me."

Without saying a word, Rashad simply followed Melissa's instructions. His anticipation grew more intense and he soon found himself struggling to control his thoughts as he envisioned himself making love to her. All he could imagine was how wonderful it would feel to be inside of her and how grateful he would be if she seduced him. This had been a recurring thought since the moment he first laid eyes on her. As he lie on the table wearing only a towel, again he allowed his eyes to close as his muscular body slowly began to relax.

In the midst of wondering what was in store for him, Rashad had been so consumed by his thoughts that he failed to notice when the lights dimmed. Moments later, he felt the warm sensation of heated oil trickling all over his back before Melissa's smooth soft hands began massaging it in.

"You like that?" she asked in a girl-like voice.

"I love it," he said without opening his eyes.

"Good. I'm glad to hear that. I told you that I wanted to do something special for you," she said as her hands continued to slide up and down his back.

Having never experienced the pleasure of a real massage, the hot oil combined with the delicate touch of Melissa's hands proved to be more than Rashad was able to handle. He slipped deeper and deeper into ecstasy and never attempted to open his eyes as the tips of Melissa's long fingernails deeply penetrated the nerves along his spine—causing him great embarrassment when he suddenly realized that he had an erection. Feeling his senses awakening throughout his body, Rashad's eyes flew open just in time to catch a glimpse of the bathrobe Melissa had changed into gently slip from her shoulders and onto the floor. He rolled over onto his back, assisting her as she climbed on top of him then watched intently as her tiny hands began exploring his protruding muscles, sending tiny chills throughout his entire body as he eagerly enjoyed every minute of it. He leaned forward and kissed Melissa passionately on the mouth, letting his hands wander wherever they pleased before cupping her buttocks and pulling her closer to him.

"Make love to me," she whispered before sucking his earlobe inside her mouth. "I need to feel you inside of me. Don't half-step either, I need you to give me everything you got."

Without hesitating, Rashad yanked his towel open and tossed it onto the floor, no longer embarrassed about her seeing his erection. A condom was the farthest thing from his mind when he placed his hand around the base of his manhood then pushed it gently inside of her vagina's opening. He could feel the walls of her vagina pulsating and throbbing as it secreted juices that seemed to be as thick and sweet as warm honey. Suddenly, Melissa's pussy came alive, suctioning his dick like a suction cup—swallowing every inch of his thick penis as she slid up and down his entire shaft. Like a dog in heat, Rashad responded by rolling Melissa onto her back, placed her legs over his shoulders then began thrusting forward with so much force that the table beneath them nearly crumbled. He pumped furiously between Melissa's legs for nearly an hour while sweating profusely and he continued to do so until he released his seed deep inside of her.

Acting as though he was really a beast, Rashad's body slumped down on the table beside Melissa's and he laid there panting before he spoke, "Damn baby, is it my birthday or is it yours?" he said, smiling. "I could be wrong, but it feels like I just gave you a gift on my birthday."

Melissa smiled at Rashad's statement as she placed her hand between her legs to feel herself, "You did put it down, baby."

"Did I?"

"Yes, you did and I don't think that I've ever had it like that before."

"Stop playing," he said before laughing. "My ego is fine, Melissa, but I do appreciate what you're trying to do."

"Oh, so you think I'm trying to stroke your ego?" she said while staring at him.

Hearing the seriousness in her voice, Rashad thought for a moment before replying, "With the games women play these days, I don't think you can blame me for not taking you seriously."

"I'm not talking about other women, Rashad! I'm talking about me, and I'm telling you, I really enjoyed the way you handled your business."

"Well, okay if you say so," he said as he toyed with her. "You told me to give it everything I had. Is it safe to assume you got what you wanted?"

"I did," she smiled. "I guess you would have to be a woman to really understand what I mean by that."

"Nope. I'll have to pass on that. I can't have nobody plunging in and out of me."

"You just don't know what you're missing," she laughed.

"I intend to keep missing it, too," he shot back. "The only thing I'm missing right now is you."

As they kissed each other passionately, Melissa felt an itching inside of her that she never felt before, and she was more than eager for Rashad to scratch it. She reached down and began fondling his genitals to arouse him. Once his manhood was fully erect, she slid from beneath him and stood on the floor, bent over the table before whispering, "Alright, baby. Let's do this again, but this time I want it from the back."

CHAPTER 6

With the State of Nevada growing at such a rapid rate, the city of Las Vegas had a lot more criminals to contain—it seemed construction was being done on every other corner. The Clark County Detention Center had opened its newly-built South Tower, which doubled the jail's population, which in turn overflooded the courts. For this reason, the Regional Justice Center, which contained three times as many courtrooms as the Clark County Courthouse, had been built to help keep things running as smoothly as possible. Paige Goldwyn sat crying in court after preliminary hearing, trying to comprehend why the justice court judge bounded her over for trial. Not once did she look back at her daughters who were also in the courtroom, she sat at the table just nodding her head before turning to her attorney with tears in her eyes, "Why am I staying in jail until trial?" she asked while reaching for a Kleenex to wipe her eyes. "Why can't you make them give me a bail?"

"Paige, we've already discussed this issue more than once," her attorney replied, trying to muster as much compassion as he possibly could. "You have to keep in mind that you're charged with murder, and from my experience, it's basically procedure that murder cases are bounded over to district court to stand trial," he continued. "Since you didn't waive your right to a speedy trial, by law, the state has to try you within sixty days. If you want, I can file another motion asking for bail, even though I doubt very seriously we'll prevail on it."

"It wouldn't hurt to try," she said sadly.

While jotting a note to himself, attorney Donald Brown found himself regretting the gesture he'd offered because he didn't think it would be wise to refile the motion, "I'll prepare it and have it filed today. If we're unsuccessful this time around, since you've held up pretty good so far, I need you to continue to do that for me."

"I'll do my best," she said while shrugging her shoulders. "When are you coming to see me again?"

"I'll try to make it down to the jail Wednesday or Thursday," he answered honestly. "More than likely it'll probably be Thursday because I have a pretty busy schedule for the next couple of days."

Paige appeared to be frustrated since it was only Monday. She rolled her eyes then crossed her arms and looked directly into his eyes before speaking, "I don't understand why Detective Bruno comes to visit me more than my own attorney."

"Paige, I come down to see you when I need to see you. Would you prefer that I come visit you when it's totally unnecessary, or would you rather I stay at my office and work on your case?" he asked while folding his arms.

"I don't really know what to say about Detective Bruno. He didn't say anything to hurt you during today's testimony but it's definitely abnormal for him to be visiting with you. I honestly don't know what to think about it."

Shortly after the brief meeting that she had with her attorney, Paige Goldwyn was removed from the courtroom by a transport officer and taken back to the jail where she remained until she went to trial. Not much had been presented during the preliminary hearing. The only witnesses who were called by the state to testify, was the emergency dispatcher who had received the 911 call, Detective Frank Bruno, and a few uniformed officers who were at the crime scene. Although she had an alibi for the time of the murder, Paige Goldwyn's attorney was not allowed to present a defense for her—they were forced to wait until trial began.

Outside of the Las Vegas Metropolitan Police Department, Detective Frank Bruno was leaving the station when he was pulled aside by Officer Jack Graham.

"You're just the man I was hoping to see," the officer said as he removed his shades.

"Jack, I'm off the clock so make it quick," the detective said while checking his watch.

"What's the deal with this Goldwyn case?"

"What do you mean?"

"I received a call from District Attorney Ricardo Burch this afternoon and he wanted to know why we didn't recover a weapon?"

"What does he mean, why?" asked the detective. "Did you tell that idiot because we couldn't find it?"

"Of course I did, Frank, but he also wanted to know why I failed to conduct a gunpowder residue test on Mrs. Goldwyn."

"Jack, why is he calling you with these questions?"

"Because, Frank, I'm the arresting officer," he said with frustration. "I wanted to perform that test on Mrs. Goldwyn, but your intervention prevented me from doing so. You said that you had it all under control so I assumed you'd do it when you were down at the jail speaking with her."

Jack Graham remembers the time when he first met the detective. He seemed to have a lot of influence and all of the other officers looked up to him. Out of the two dozen officers who were new to the force—fresh out of the police academy, it was he whom the detective had taken under his wing and sent out on the beat with four experienced officers to get his first experience of on-the-job-training. He'll always remember that terrible night. The memory will forever be embedded in his mind—as if he was under Murphy's Law, whatever could go wrong, did go wrong.

It was five of them total. He and four other officers had piled into a paddy wagon responding to a domestic disturbance call when he found himself in a foot pursuit. An older black guy with a long history of domestic violence had assaulted his wife of many years and was trying to get away when the police arrived. Wanting to prove himself to the other officers, it was he who had managed to catch up with the suspect—finding himself in a tense wrestling match as the perpetrator refused to be taken down easily. Managing to get behind the suspect, he placed his baton against the man's throat—held it tightly on both ends while pulling his weight backwards until they both fell. Using all of his might to hold the baton in place, Officer Jack Graham could only stare at the overcast as he pleaded with the suspect to give up when his fellow officers arrived on the scene.

"Stop Resisting!" an officer yelled before kicking the suspect across the face.

The officers arrived in tandem, each one yelled stop resisting as they kicked and stomped the unarmed suspect. Officer Jack Graham was surprised. Although he knew that the vicious beating was uncalled for, he could only watch as he crawled from the ground and holstered his baton while his fellow colleagues continued to yell stop resisting. They beat the man until they killed him, and there was nothing Jack Graham could do about it. Watching a man get beat to death in cold blood was a hard pill to swallow. He didn't understand what happened or why it happened until he was pulled aside by his fellow officers when they cooked up a story for internal affairs. That's when Officer Jack Graham learned that 'stop resisting' wasn't meant for the suspect at all. It was the officer's way of communicating to each other, letting each other know to use excessive force. A police code—one of many used by law enforcement. Officer Jack Graham knew it wasn't right but it explained everything he had witnessed that fatal evening. He found himself at the mercy of internal affairs, even though all of the officers on the scene corroborated each other's story—the one they made up after the incident. Internal Affairs made things hard for him—real hard. Watching every move he made and caused him to feel uncomfortable in his own skin. After two months, he wanted to just throw in the towel and quit the police force, until suddenly, the investigation abruptly ended. The Internal Affairs' investigation was officially over and he's grateful to the detective for coming to his aid. He doesn't know which department head the man spoke with or what was said, but the investigation was discontinued and he credits Detective Bruno for making it happen.

Now, Officer Jack Graham found himself feeling guilty. Knowing he was in violation for questioning Detective Bruno's expertise, who in fact was the same man who'd saved him from internal affairs. He assessed the situation then eased up a bit as he held his tongue and listened intently.

"Jack, the next time someone calls you asking questions about this case, you make sure you tell them to call me. I'm the one in charge of this investigation and they should call me before calling anyone else, you got that?"

"I got it," the officer replied.

"Good," he said while adjusting his belt. "All protocol was followed in this case, and if anyone has questions they should come to me."

"Okay, Frank, I got it. I understand."

"You better, because I don't want to hear no more about it," he said before walking off.

CHAPTER 7

It was a long busy day at the massage parlor, but it finally managed to drag itself to an end. The four women weren't ready to call it a night, so instead of ending it by going home, they chose to relax at a nearby pub. It was a place that they'd frequented several times before—but what still remained fresh in all of their minds was an incident that happened two weeks before. Melissa drank more alcohol than she was able to handle, and had urinated and vomited all over herself as she sat at a table in front of the bar. When the bartender refused to keep serving her drinks, she became so infuriated that she had to be subdued by two other patrons after throwing an empty shot-glass at the bartender's head. Although she missed, they all knew that she could have easily been arrested for public intoxication if he hadn't been persuaded not to press any charges. Embarrassed by what Melissa had done, Michelle, Meagan and Alix, all pitched in and gave the man a hundred dollars apiece then apologized repeatedly for Melissa's behavior.

As they all sat fretting about how tired they were, three of the women were still sipping their first cocktail, unlike Melissa who was sipping her third. Having only been there for a half an hour, Michelle, Meagan and Alix quickly realized that Melissa was drinking too much so they all agreed that it was best to leave. The twins only lived a few blocks away from the pub, so instead of taking a chance on Melissa getting too drunk; they made a conscious decision to go chill at their place.

Wearing an all white miniskirt with a matching top, Melissa climbed in on the passenger's side of Alix's SUV and nearly fell backwards as she told Meagan to ride with Michelle in the Range Rover.

"You should throw that drink away, Melissa," Alix suggested.

"Throw it away for what?" said Melissa as she struggled to fasten her seat belt.

"I don't like driving with open containers in my car," Alix replied.

"I didn't buy it to throw away. I could have finished it inside the bar, but since everyone wanted to leave so early, I'll just go ahead and finish it now."

"I'm just trying to look out for you," Alix said as she pulled off. "I can see what's happening to you, Melissa, and I hope you can stop it before it's too late."

Trying not to spit out the contents she sipped from her glass, Melissa placed a firm hand over her mouth then tilted her head backwards and began laughing, "What do you think is happening to me, Alix?"

"You're turning into an alcoholic."

"Your opinion don't mean shit," she stated calmly.

"I hope it does."

"Well, since we all have to be something, I guess I'm cool with being an alcoholic. I'd rather be that than the bullshit you represent," Melissa said as she took another sip.

"What's that supposed to mean?" Alix laughed.

"Well, I could call you a whore, but I won't do that because I understand."

"A whore?" Alix asked, surprised. "If I recall correctly, Melissa, you're the slut who sucked your boyfriend's dick and fucked him while you were on the job? I'm the one who owns the place and I've never even done anything like that."

"That doesn't make me a whore!" Melissa shot back. "I'm a smart bitch, and I only did what any smart bitch would do to please her man on his birthday," she said with her words slurring. "Damn right I hooked him up for his birthday, but it's not like I would do it for just anybody. Look at you. As often as Mark's old ass comes to the parlor, don't act like you've never done that shit for him."

"I'm sorry, but Mark and I don't have that kind of relationship. We're only friends," Alix explained. "Since he gave me the money to open the parlor, we agreed from the very beginning that he could come in as often as he likes and I will always give him a free massage. That's all there is between Mark and I."

"Not even once?" Melissa asked, curiosity getting the best of her.

"Never!" said Alix. "That man couldn't tell you shit about this pussy.

Did you really think I was sleeping with him?"

"I did. I think Michelle and Meagan think so, too."

"Mark suffers from erectile dysfunction. He can't get it up and he told me that when we first met. Even if he could though, he couldn't handle this pussy even if somebody else was helping him," Alix giggled.

Melissa laughed while downing the last of her drink then unlatched her seat belt before speaking, "He's just a sugar daddy, huh? A sugar daddy who isn't getting any."

"I wouldn't call him a sugar daddy. If anything he's more like a father-figure," Alix said as she pulled into the driveway and parked behind the Range Rover.

Once they were inside, Alix joined Michelle and Meagan who were sprawled across the living room couch. Melissa paid no attention to what they were doing; she headed straight to the bar to fix her a drink.

"Damn, this girl acts like she can't go a few minutes without having a drink," Michelle yelled.

"That's exactly what I told her on the way over here," Alix added.

Melissa tried her best to ignore the comments but her anger soon got the best of her, "Here we go with this shit again," she said before pausing. "Why is it that every time I turn around somebody is always complaining about what I'm doing? I'm just trying to do me—I'm not hurtin' no fuckin' body."

"Melissa. Never mind," Alix said with frustration. "Meagan, I think we should go. It's getting late and you know we all have work tomorrow."

As Meagan and Alix got up to leave, Melissa angrily slammed her glass on top of the bar before storming up the stairs and into her bedroom.

"Don't worry about her, she'll be okay," Michelle said while looking toward the staircase.

"She needs to realize that she has a problem," Alix said in a low voice. "We'll see you in the morning, Michelle, and hopefully Melissa will be okay by then."

"I'm sure she will," Michelle whispered as she fought back tears. "Goodnight you guys. Send me a text message when you make it home."

"I will," said Meagan.

As they walked down the driveway toward the SUV, Meagan and Alix both voiced their opinions about what should be done about Melissa's behavior, "I would hate to have to fire her, but she'll leave me no choice if she keeps this up," Alix said as she used her remote to unlock the doors.

Inside the house, the twins had no clue what Alix was thinking. They sat in their bedrooms upset with each other—each forming different opinions about what had transpired a few moments before. Michelle was in a daze, wondering how she could help her sister, but receiving help seemed to be the farthest thing from Melissa's mind. She lay fully clothed across her bed, head resting on her arm before reaching for her cell phone to place a call.

Amp opened the front door to let Chyna inside before returning to his spot on the black leather sofa. He had been sitting in the same spot for nearly an hour watching *America's Most Wanted*—a television series he had grown to appreciate after his ten year old son was shot to death on Halloween night a few years earlier, "Oh, I'm sorry. Can I get you something to drink?" he asked after sitting back down and grabbing the remote control.

"No, I'm fine," Chyna replied as she plopped down on the couch. "I just had the strangest thing happen to me."

"What happened?" asked Amp.

"I went on a call at the Venetian Hotel, and this guy—I think he's from London or Argentina somewhere, didn't want to have sex with me, didn't want a hand job, oral sex or anything. All this guy wanted me to do was spank his bare ass with my hand as hard as I could and yell at him— telling him how naughty he's been. He was moaning as I did this to him until he ended up squirting all over himself. It was crazy," she said, smiling.

All Amp could do was laugh, "I've heard some weird stories in my life but I have never heard of no shit like that. But, then again, that's why companies like TopNotch Entertainment continue to exist. Whatever a man can't get his woman to do at home, he know he can always count on people like me to send him a girl who'll happily fulfill whatever fantasies or fetishes he may have. No matter how kinky it is. If he got the money, we'll accommodate him," he said confidently.

Chyna pulled a wad of cash from inside of her bra and showed it to Amp before uttering, "He paid me a thousand dollars, and I'll do it again if he wants me to."

Amp had really grown to like Chyna. She wasn't the most beautiful of the six girls he and Bull employed, but, to him, being Chinese and black made her the most exotic. He thought of her as a hot commodity. Her sexily slanted eyes, long black hair, and slender physique, quickly proved to be very lucrative for he and Bull's escort service. He really enjoyed her company and he hung out with her as often as possible. Unlike his comrade, Bull, Amp never had sex with any of the girls who worked for him. He believed in keeping business and pleasure separate, and that probably explains how he remained successful, "How long do you plan on staying in this business, Chyna?" he asked suddenly.

"I don't know, I've never really thought about it," she said as she checked her email, using her cell phone. "I'm only twenty-two, I love the money—so I'll probably do this until I'm around thirty."

"Then what?" he asked curiously.

"Then, maybe I'll get married and start a family," she said sincerely. "I've always wanted to have a baby; I've just been wanting to wait until the time was right."

"I think that'll be good for you. You're a good girl and I think you'll make a good mom."

"Thank you, Anthony. I really appreciate that," she said enthused. "Every time we talk, you always have something positive to say to me. That's why I love talking to you because you always say something to lift my spirits."

"I take that as a compliment," Amp replied. "Instead of being so quick to tear people down, I believe it's imperative to lift people up. I'm not saying it just to be saying it though, I truly believe that you'll make a great mom," he said convincingly.

"That's exactly what I mean," Chyna replied. "Doing what I do for a living, people tend to look down on me and you're the only one who never does that. You actually give me compliments," she paused, hoping not to cry. "You know, every time I get ready to go on a call, I try to always look and smell good—hoping the guy will give me a compliment—but when I get to his room, the same thing always happens. He looks at me like I'm damaged goods, barks all these orders at me, and expects me to just perform for him. It never fails. No compliments or anything," she said with tears in her eyes. "I'm a woman, a human being and we all like to be complimented sometimes."

"Come here and give me a hug," Amp said while reaching for her. "Chyna, you're too beautiful to be upset about something like this. Don't let the people in this world get the best of you. You have to always believe in yourself. It doesn't matter what anyone else thinks of you, whether they compliment you or not, as long as you know you're beautiful, it doesn't matter what anyone else thinks. Your opinion about yourself is all that matters."

"I know," she forced a smile. "And, I apologize for being so sensitive."

"Don't worry about it," Amp assured her. "You're human, and there's nothing wrong with expressing your feelings. Regardless of your line of work, you still have a right to express yourself."

"That's why I love talking to you, Anthony. No matter how bad I feel, you never fail to put a smile on my face. You need to teach Bull a thing or two, he could definitely use a lesson on how to treat women," they both laughed. "Where is he anyway? I saw his car parked outside."

Not really wanting to answer the question, Amp thought for a moment before speaking, "Upstairs doing what he do best."

"That's all he does is have sex," said Chyna. "It's not me so it must be Veronica or Jazmin, or is it Amanda?"

"Nope," he said, smiling.

"Missy or Kim?" she continued guessing.

"Nope."

"Who is it then?" she persisted.

"You wouldn't believe me if I told you."

"Amp, who is it?" she begged.

"He got one of the twins up there from next door. She called here drunk a lil' earlier and he somehow talked her into coming over."

"Does she do X?"

"I don't know, but she's been up there with him for a long time."

Chyna left ten minutes later. Amp thought about going to Bull's bedroom to make sure he and Melissa was okay, but decided against it almost immediately. He jumped into his red new-model Porsche, made his way onto the freeway ramp—destined to go check things out at TopNotch Entertainment.

CHAPTER 8

Just like all the other mornings in the county jail, the D-module workers on the third floor was all set up for breakfast by five AM. In the control booth, a short female guard stood in front of the control panel with her hands on her hips, as she waited for the hand-signal from the two module workers, to start opening doors so the women could eat. What the guard didn't know was that tension between two female inmates had been brewing overnight because of words they exchanged the evening before. While standing at their doors waiting to disperse from their cells, Tangie Robinson slowly paced back and forth inside of her cell with her fists clenched tightly, mumbling under her breath. Moments later, the entire day-room quickly flooded with women after the guard received the signal from one of the module workers. It looked like a scene from the Kentucky Derby when horses broke from their gates simultaneously.

Instead of systematically lining up in front of the breakfast cart, Tangie took advantage of the opportunity and ran into the cell and blocked the door of the woman she had been arguing with the night before. The fight was on. Using all of the strength that they could muster, both women were eagerly at each other's throats, swinging violently inside of the small dark cell, trying everything they could to hurt one another, "Bitch, you think you're tough, huh?" Tangie asked, sensing that she had finally met her match.

"I'll show you better than I can tell you."

"You gon' have to show me then, bitch, 'cause I don't believe you."

The women faced each other head-on. They were evenly matched, neither wanting to back down as they kicked, scratched and clawed each other. Meanwhile, the guard inside the control booth still had no clue what was taking place. Luckily, the breakfast line hadn't fully diminished, so the two women involved in the altercation were able to slip out of the cell without being detected. Although they were both heaving heavily trying to catch their breath, they casually strode through the line and grabbed their trays then made their way to their tables like nothing had happened. Once they sat down and began eating, the rest of the women inside the module were all secretly staring trying to see who'd won.

Tangie Robinson was a thick black woman in her mid-thirties who was well known for being tough and openly gay. She was also known for being quick to stick her nose in other people's business, which was a definite no-no, especially in jail.

As they sat at their tables—appearing to be calm, neither woman knew what the other was thinking as they stared at each other from across the module. Subsequently, the other women talked quietly amongst themselves, purposely looking at Paige with a newfound respect. Not only had she stood up to Tangie Robinson, but it was clear to everyone in the module that the beautiful petite blonde had held her own.

A few hours later, once everything had been cleaned up by the module workers, the women inside the D-module were all let out of their cells for morning's free-time. This was their time to shower, use the phone, read the daily newspaper, socialize, or do whatever they wanted in the spacious day-room. Since Paige and Tangie had fought hours earlier, the tension hung over the module like thick smoke, causing everyone to feel the slight discomfort. No one readily engaged in their daily routine, instead, the majority of the women stood hanging around, anxiously waiting to see if something else would spark. On a normal day, the only thing usually on Paige's mind was to use the phone to check on things at home. This morning was different. Sporting a newly-bruised eye, she failed to show any sign of weakness as she dragged a chair to the back of the module and sat next to an older woman she had grown to like, "Hey, Chrissy," she said in a sweet voice.

"Good morning, champ," Chrissy said jokingly. "Aren't you gonna call your daughters this morning?"

"Nah, I think I'll wait until this afternoon," Paige replied.

Chrissy Hicks was a well-known Vegas madam who had been in and out of state and federal prison since age nineteen. Now at age fifty-five, many women found themselves drawn to her because she was known for being wise and gave good advice.

Suddenly, as if something terrible was about to happen, everything was reduced to silence as Tangie approached the two women in the back of the module, "Good morning, ladies," she said as she pulled up a chair.

"What's up, Tangie?" Chrissy replied.

"Paige, I just wanted to apologize to you for what happened this morning," Tangie said politely. "Whatever happened between you and your husband is none of my business, and I was totally out of line for asking you about it."

With no immediate response, Tangie was unsure how to react when Paige sat there staring without saying anything, "Apology accepted," she finally said.

"I have to commend you for standing up for yourself, and I hope that we can be cool from this point on," said Tangie.

"We're cool," Paige said as they shook hands.

As Tangie turned on her heels and walked away, the rest of the women inside the module were in disbelief about what they'd witnessed. Tangie Robinson had beaten up plenty of women since being in jail, and not once, had she apologized to any of them or came anywhere close to admitting she was wrong. Rather surprised by the sudden apology, Paige turned to Chrissy expecting an answer but, she too, appeared to be just as shocked.

"It took a lot of courage for her to tell you that, and you should honor it by accepting it and letting it go," she said in a serious tone. "There's no need to think about it no more and don't let these messy women in here trick you into talking about it," she continued. "It's behind you now and it's up to you to keep it that way."

Taking heed to what Chrissy had said, Paige was elated to have her differences with Tangie resolved. It crossed her mind to call her daughters, but her thought was soon interrupted when she was called upstairs for a legal visit.

"Good morning, Mrs. Goldwyn, how is everything?" the detective asked as soon as she sat down.

"I'm fine, Frank. Just another day in the county jail," said Paige.

Noticing the eminent swelling and discoloration, the detective leaned back in his chair and seemed to be quite alarmed when he spoke again, "What happened to your eye?"

"Oh, it's nothing, just irritated from me rubbing it," she lied quickly.

As if they were on the same side of the law, Detective Frank Bruno and Paige Goldwyn had developed a very unique friendship since she'd been in jail. Viewed by many of his colleagues as inappropriate, the handsome homicide detective had taken a liking to the beautiful murder-suspect and had made up several excuses for why he needed to see her.

"What brings you here so early, detective?" she asked while staring at him.

"Well, with your case going to trial in a couple of weeks, there's something that's kind of been bothering me."

"What's wrong?" Paige asked, sensing that there was something he really wanted to say to her.

"Well, for one, I don't understand why you would hire a black attorney to represent you when the victim in your case is African-American," he said before clearing his throat. "You need to find out what his plans are because these people have a tendency to side with each other," he went on.

"Since it's probably too late to hire a white attorney, I think you would be a lot better off if your lawyer keeps as many whites on the jury as possible—white men in particular," he concluded.

Paige was shocked by the blunt remark, so she said the first thing that came to her mind, "Is this what you came to talk to me about?"

"It may not seem important to you right now, but the jury you end up with is key in this case," he said with his arms crossed. "I'm sure your attorney knows the importance of this but you should ask to be sure, because if he doesn't, you'll be the one who'll suffer because of it."

"Detective, it has really been a tough day for me and I really don't feel like hearing this crap," she stated frankly. "I do appreciate your concern though, and I will be sure to ask my attorney about it."

"Okay, babe," he said as he realized the words that came from his mouth.

Detective Bruno stood up to leave but he turned around as soon as he reached the door, "I'm sorry, Mrs. Goldwyn if I offended you, but I wanted to make sure that you were aware of this."

"Yeah right," said Paige.

Once the meeting was over, Paige was pat-searched by a masculine-looking female officer before heading downstairs to her housing unit. In her mind, she knew that the detective was racist, but there was something about him that appealed to her. As she thought back to the day when she was arrested, she recalled the unmistakable desire she'd seen in his eyes when she was being escorted to the police car. She knew from that moment he was attracted to her, and her early suspicions had just been confirmed. As her mind replayed everything he'd said, there was no mistaking the lust he had in his eyes when he had actually slipped and called her babe.

Hours later, at an upscale restaurant in the Seven Hills section of Las Vegas, Detective Frank Bruno invited himself to a corner booth that was already occupied by two other men.

"Howdy, Frank, how's it going?" said the older of the two men. "What brings you to this neck of the woods?"

"Ah, just following a lead in a case I'm working on, but I got a little famish, so here I am," he replied as he sat down. "How have you been, Carl? It's been a while since we've seen each other."

"Try telling that to the DA's office, maybe they'll give me some time off," the men laughed.

"I know what you mean," the detective replied. "I think we all could use some time off. Don't feel bad, though. Working for metro is just as bad as working for the DA's office."

"Not necessarily," the older man said. "All you guys do is make arrests—then leave us stuck doing mountains of paperwork trying to figure out the validity of the arrests you've made. I think my job is a little more tedious than yours. If you don't believe me, let's trade for a week," he said as they laughed again.

"I think I'll pass," replied the detective. "Carl, are you the one handling the Goldwyn case?"

"No, I think Burch is handling that one."

"He has his work cut out for him. Now, if anyone in your office is going to complain about something, he's the one who has a reason to," the detective said.

"Burch has a lot of experience, so I'm pretty sure he'll be okay. He's the best we've got," the older man said.

"How would one go about defending a case like this when there's not much evidence to rely upon?" asked the detective.

"Frank, you've been in law enforcement for a long time. We all have, and you know we can't discuss anything like that with you," the older man explained.

Detective Bruno suddenly seemed to lose interest, "Since no one has come to take my order, I may as well go ahead and pursue this lead," he said as he rose to his feet. "Carl, it was nice seeing you again and I hope it doesn't take so long to see you again."

"Take care, Frank, and try not to work too hard," Carl replied.

"Sorry, I didn't catch your name," he said to the younger man who hadn't said a word the entire time.

"Steve."

"Nice to meet you, Steve," he said as he shook his hand then made his departure.

Anyone who spent time in law enforcement knew that the upscale restaurant in Seven Hills was a known hangout spot for district attorneys. It's where they socialized every day. So, for Frank Bruno to pop up the way he did, the two DA's he encountered were certain that there was a reason behind it, so they chose to be reticent and played it safe. They both had their suspicions about why he had come, but neither man spoke openly about what he thought.

The men gathered in front of the run-down porch, watching as the suspicious vehicle slowly crept to a halt before turning into the parking lot of the small duplex.

"Excuse me, is this the Clark residence?" the man asked as he let down his window. "I'm looking for a Ms. Shafora Clark, do you know her?"

"Oh yeah, that's my homegirl she live right here," the stranger said while pointing to the apartment.

The man climbed out of the luxury SUV, toting what appeared to be a satchel as he adjusted the jacket of his expensive suit. Normally he was confident, but since he found himself in a neighborhood that he was unfamiliar with, he found it somewhat hard to keep his bearings, "How are you gentlemen?" he said as he approached the porch.

"We're alright," the man said, cautiously. He seemed to be the spokesperson or the one in charge because the other two men never said a word. "Can I ask what you want with Shafora. She's not in any trouble, is she?"

"None that I know of," the man replied. "I'm Attorney Donald Brown and I'm here to ask Ms. Clark some questions."

"Oh, okay," the man said as he stepped aside. "I'm not trying to be nosy or nothin', I'm just trying to look out for my homegirl."

"Understandable," the attorney said as he pushed past the man then knocked on the door. He stood in wonderment, not knowing what to expect when he heard footsteps approaching from the other side.

"Hello, you must be Mr. Brown?" the woman said with a smile, immediately realizing that she wasn't appropriately dressed.

"And you must be Ms. Clark?" he said as he stepped inside then closed the door behind him.

"I am, but call me Shafora. My mother Rose Marie Clark is the only one who deserves to be called Mrs. Clark."

"I respect that. Would it be okay if I sit down?"

"Sure, go ahead," said Shafora. "I apologize for the way I'm dressed but I had just gotten out of the shower when you knocked on the door."

"That's not a problem," he said as if he hadn't noticed that she was only wrapped in a towel. "I shouldn't be too long; I only have a few things that I need to ask you about."

"I see you got past my watchdogs," she said while smiling.

"I don't recall seeing any dogs."

"The three dudes you saw out there," she said as she smiled harder.

"Oh, them?" he laughed. "At first I was a little skeptical, but they turned out to be well-behaved. Are they friends of yours?"

"They are now," she said after thinking about it. "Actually, they were good friends with my ex, but since we broke up—they never stopped hanging around, even though he doesn't come around no more."

"You're referring to Marcus, right?"

"Yes. Marcus, M-80, whichever one you prefer to call him."

At that instant, a woman came into the living room from the hallway and approached Shafora—embracing her from the back. She was also only wearing a towel and kissed Shafora on the neck very affectionately, "This must be the lawyer you were expecting?"

"Uh-huh," Shafora replied in a soft voice. "This is Attorney Donald Brown. Mr. Brown this is my baby, Charmain."

"Hello," he said as Charmain waved using only her fingers, both women could tell that he was caught off guard.

Charmain smiled to herself as she strode sexily up the hallway, leaving the attorney and her girlfriend to resume their meeting in private.

"Now, where were we?" said Shafora before leaning against the couch across from him.

"Hmm, I think we were on the subject of Marcus, but I didn't get a chance to ask you what kind of guy he was."

"What kind of guy he was or what kind of boyfriend he was to me?"

"It wouldn't hurt to hear both," the attorney said.

Taking a moment to cogitate, Shafora placed her hand underneath her chin then looked down at the floor before she spoke, "He's like two different people," she said before pausing. "When we first met, he was a dream-come-true, but he turned out to be a nightmare."

"How so?"

"Well, for one, he used to kick my ass," she said emphatically. "I hated Marcus as a boyfriend. The way he treated me, the way he talked to me—he made me feel like I was less than human."

"How long were you two together?"

"Only for a few months, but with all the riff-raff in our relationship, it seemed like we were together for twenty years!"

"That bad, huh?" the attorney asked.

"It wasn't cool at all," she said as she shook her head. "That's why I turned to women. Once I was done with Marcus, I swore to never fuck with a man again. Excuse my language, but I get mad every time I think about that motherfucker. To me, that dude is a bitch and I can't help the way I feel about him."

"I'm sorry to hear you feel like that, Ms. Clark."

"Shafora," she reminded him.

"That's right, Shafora," he smiled. "It saddens me to hear that you feel like that. Didn't you say there were two sides of him?"

"You have the good Marcus and the bad M-80. He was two people in one and I believe I was mostly dealing with M-80. On the other hand, he loved his homeboys. He was as loyal as they come when it came to his so-called gang. I mean, I was his girl, but he put his homies before he put me."

"Is he still part of a gang?"

"No, not anymore," she said seriously. "Marcus has not been around here in a minute. This is their so-called 'hood and his homies haven't seen or heard from him."

"Are the guys outside gang members?" the attorney asked with a concerned look.

"Yes, they are," she smiled. "They are all Hoover Crips just like

Marcus, but like I said, he has not been around here in a long time. I hear he lives on 28th Street, though."

"Who told you that?"

"Bullet."

"Bullet?" the attorney shrugged.

"You just met him outside; he was standing right there when I opened the door for you. He's their so-called shot-caller; he's probably the one who did all the talking."

"The one who referred to you as his homegirl?"

"Yeah, him," she smiled. "He's been calling me that ever since I started dealing with Marcus. He's a pretty good guy, though. He even pulled Marcus off me a couple times when he was jumping on me for no fuckin' reason. Now he's just over-protective—he don't want nobody getting close to me."

"That explains why he gave me the third-degree," said the attorney.

Shafora smiled. It made her feel good to know that Bullet was protective of her.

"Well, I guess I better be going," he said as he stood up. "Thank you, Shafora for the information—it was a great pleasure meeting you."

"The pleasure was all mine," she replied.

When he reached the door, a thought occurred to the defense attorney so he looked over his shoulder in Shafora's direction, "Does it bother you to know that these gentlemen are still hanging around your apartment even though you and Marcus aren't together anymore."

"Well, to be honest, this is their 'hood and they were actually here before I moved in," she said.

"Okay then, since they're so familiar with you, I need to ask a favor of you. Can you watch to make sure I get to my car safely?"

"Sure," she said. She laughed when she realized the man was serious.

CHAPTER 9

Shortly after four AM Tuesday morning, Michelle Goldwyn lay wide awake as she heard noise coming from Melissa's bedroom. She had been awakened by it several times throughout the night and was becoming more upset at her sister's behavior. Since they both had to get up in a couple of hours, she decided she'd ease her frustration before going to work by relaxing her mind with a soothing bath. She forced herself to climb out of bed, slipped out of her pajamas and bikini panties then threw her long terry cloth bathrobe over her shoulders. When she stepped out of her bedroom and into the hallway, everything was dark and quiet except for the sounds that crept from her sister's bedroom. Trying desperately to ignore the sounds, Michelle quickly succumbed to the increasing pressure as curiosity easily got the best of her. She tiptoed in the direction that the sounds were coming from, inched her way closer and closer—finally reaching the door before pressing her ear gently against it. She placed her hand on her sister's doorknob, held her breath as she turned it slowly—heart rate dramatically increased as she cracked it open to peek inside. Once she got a glimpse of the large bed, instinctively, Michelle closed her eyes then clamped her hand over her mouth when she saw her sister lying naked on top of the covers. Melissa was screaming into a pillow with her legs spread widely apart—draped over Rashad's shoulders as his body slammed violently into hers. Michelle soon realized that what had been keeping her awake throughout the night was the sound of the headboard hitting the wall. Quietly, she pulled the door shut, eased her hand from the knob and no longer had the urge to take a bath. Infuriated by what she'd seen, she went into her bedroom and closed the door—still sporting her long bathrobe with nothing underneath when she jumped into bed and dozed off. She woke up a couple hours later, took a shower and got dressed before heading downstairs where Melissa was humming.

"Good morning, sis," Melissa said cheerfully.

Not wanting to lose her temper, Michelle suppressed her anger before replying, "Why are you all bright-eyed and bushy-tailed? You must have already had your drink this morning?"

"Why does it always have to come to this?" said Melissa. "Every time you see me in a good mood you automatically assume that I've been drinking."

"Well, what is it then?" Michelle continued. "Is it alcohol, or is it the company you had last night that got you down here in such a good mood?"

"No, that's not it," said Melissa.

"You didn't have company last night?" Michelle asked, knowing damn well her sister was lying.

"No, I didn't! And, why is my business so important to you?"

"Why the fuck are you lying, Melissa? You and Rashad kept me up all night with that bullshit! I don't know why you're still messing around with him when you know all he wants is sex from you."

"You're just jealous 'cause don't nobody want sex from you."

"Don't be stupid, Melissa. Rashad's brother has torn our family apart, or did you forget that?" Michelle said in a louder voice. "Melissa, while you're fucking around with Rashad, has it ever occurred to you that our dad is dead and our mom is in jail for what his stupid ass brother has done?"

Melissa paused then bit her lip and stared down at the floor before replying, "I think about it sometimes, but it doesn't affect me the way it affects you. I don't let it get to me like that."

"Melissa, look at me," she said with anger in her voice. "How can you look at Rashad's stupid ass and still act like that shit doesn't bother you? You're still sleeping with him and inviting him over—so you must be just as stupid as him!"

"Michelle, we don't know for sure who killed our dad!" Melissa yelled back. "We can't say for certain that Marcus did it. I don't think mom did it either, but we won't know anything until she goes to trial."

"You can't be that damn stupid, Melissa? You know damn well mom is innocent. Now she's in jail fighting other women and going through all kinds of shit because of something your boyfriend's brother has done," Michelle said with her hand on her hip. "You haven't been putting money on her books, writing her or anything, but you always have money to buy alcohol and do other bullshit that doesn't mean anything. What happened to my twin sister, and where's the innocent girl I used to know?"

"I grew up," Melissa replied.

"Grew up? Bitch, you need to wake up! You have no clue that Alix is thinking about firing your ass because of your fucked up attitude. If it wasn't for me talking her out of it, she would have fired your ass a long time ago," Michelle said as tears welled in her eyes. "You know what? For us to be identical twins, we're nothing alike, and that's really sad because I miss my sister," she said before walking off.

As Melissa stood in silence cogitating for moment, she wiped a tear that fell from her eye before heading outside where Michelle was waiting. She climbed inside the Range Rover, placed her hand on her sister's leg and looked into her eyes before speaking, "Michelle, I apologize for hurting you," she said sincerely. "I give you my word, from now on, you don't ever have to worry about me drinking or doing anything that'll upset you. I'll even stop seeing Rashad if you want me to." A statement she immediately regretted, because she couldn't deny the fact that she loved his sex.

"Thank you," Michelle replied in a soft voice as she leaned forward to hug her sister. "Moms' trial begins in less than two weeks and you know she'll need us to be there for her."

"Count me in," Melissa replied.

Once the massage parlor shut its door for the evening, Meagan, Alix and the twins went out to dinner at an expensive restaurant to congratulate Melissa on her decision to change. As soon as dinner was over, the women ordered their favorite cocktails, but when the waitress asked Melissa what she wanted to drink, she kept her word and ordered a soda instead. She seemed to be serious about changing her life for the better, and what had really convinced her to make the decision was the pain she had seen in her sister's eyes. She didn't bother telling Michelle about her roll in the hay with Bull, or about the ecstasy she'd tried, and since she had no intentions of ever doing it again, she didn't feel it was necessary.

It was past midnight when Chyna entered the dark colored SUV that was parked in the parking lot of TopNotch Entertainment. She climbed in wearing a one-piece denim outfit that she hiked up around her waist as soon as she closed the passenger's side door, "Oooh, baby, I've been waiting for this moment for what seems like forever," she said as she crawled across the front seat towards the driver. "My pussy has been throbbing and dripping like crazy ever since you gave me those fuckin' pills."

Bull quickly reclined in his seat, removed the large caliber handgun that he kept in his waistband then unbuckled his pants and pulled out his manhood. Chyna leaned over his lap and greedily took his erect manhood down her throat—sucking it deeply and quickly in a smooth rhythm as Bull tightened his buttocks and enjoyed the ride. Without missing a beat, Chyna reached back and thrust two fingers deeply inside herself, trying to bring herself to orgasm, while continuing her act of oral sex. Bull was speechless. He sat there in the driver's seat clinging tightly to the steering wheel holding his mouth open until he closed his eyes and ejaculated. Chyna lapped up every drop of his steaming jism—bobbing her head up and down in a desperate attempt to get some more. She removed her fingers from her wet vagina—hungrily placed them inside her mouth, tasting her own juices as she licked each finger, moaning seductively, "Mmmm," she said with her eyes closed. "My pussy tastes sooo good, are you in the mood to lick it for me?"

"Nah, baby, not tonight," Bull replied. "I got those pills from my new connect and it looks like I've made a good investment. That shit got you horny, huh?"

"Yes, it does. My pussy feels like it's on fire," she said as she continued touching herself.

Bull wanted to spend more time with Chyna, but he couldn't, because she had to go on another call. He had recently found a new ecstasy connection, Lonnie Garner, in California and Chyna had volunteered to test the quality of the product for him. Judging from her reaction, it appeared to be potent and he had other prospects in mind who he thought would be interested in trying it. He spent the next forty-five minutes doing paperwork at TopNotch Entertainment, before heading home where Amp was waiting.

It was just past two AM when Bull entered the large house and saw Amp sitting with his head down at the kitchen table, "Amp, wake up," he said while tapping his shoulder. "I know I should have been home a couple hours ago but taking care of the books took a lil' longer than I expected."

"What time is it?" asked Amp.

"Way past your bedtime," Bull laughed. "For you to still be up this late trying to wait on me, this situation we have must be really important?"

Amp had called earlier that evening and told him that there was something very important they needed to discuss. To avoid saying the wrong thing, Amp chose his words carefully before speaking, "Bull, I think you should leave those pills alone for a while, man," he stated firmly. "You gotta stop selling 'em and using 'em until this detective leaves us the fuck alone."

"Why is he still fuckin' with us?" Bull asked. "He already know we didn't have shit to do with what happened next door."

"I don't know, but he keeps coming around the house and the business, and although everything's legit, I don't want those ecstasy pills to fuck shit up for us. You having those pills can bring a lot of heat and I would hate for him to keep snoopin' around and catch wind of it then bust in here thinking we're selling drugs. I can't be around that shit, Bull. You know my daughter will be here in a week or two and I can't have her around no shit like that."

"I understand, man," Bull replied. "This detective is pissin' me off, though. I don't think I told you about the comments that fool was making when they took my gun to run those tests. Once they realized it wasn't the weapon that killed dude, that fool said it was probably one of my homies who did it 'cause my kind have always been like crabs in a barrel. I don't know what he meant by that, but it sound like he's on some racial shit."

"That's why I'm asking you to chill out with the pills," Amp yawned. "He told me that he would have his eye on us. Said he don't understand how we could afford this house or the business, as if we shouldn't have this kind of shit. We're entitled just like he's entitled, but you know they don't like to see blacks having shit."

"He's a trip," said Bull.

"I know. That's why you gotta leave those pills alone," he repeated. "When my baby comes to live with me, I can't have her around no bullshit. She's only eight, so the girls won't be allowed over here no more either. Not as long as Jada is living here."

"It's understandable, man, and I got your point," said Bull.

"Alright, man, I'll see you in the morning."

"See you in the morning," Bull replied.

CHAPTER 10

Weekends were always the busiest at the Galleria Mall, but the weekdays produced a much calmer atmosphere. Marcus sat expressionless in the food court watching Andrea, as she scolded her daughters, Lexi and Jazzy. He loved seeing the girls play and enjoy themselves, but since there was a time and place for everything, he understood why they had to be disciplined. Shopping with a woman was something he dreaded but he enjoyed spending time with Andrea and her daughters. A few weeks back, they took a road trip to L.A. and Chicago and he sensed that Andrea wanted more from him. He loved how they interacted when they went to functions; church, dinner, museums, and movie theaters and every time they went out, they felt like family. Marcus was proud of himself for changing his lifestyle; he vowed to never again put himself in jeopardy. Andrea and her daughters meant the world to him. He was happy to be part of something he felt was important.

"Marcus, can we go to the arcade to play video games?" asked Jazzy. She was the oldest of the two girls and she rarely did anything without her younger sister.

"If your mother says it's okay, it's okay with me," said Marcus. Even though he was a father-figure to Lexi and Jazzy, he never tried to act like he was their father. Most of the time, the girls lived with their grandmother while they attended school, but whenever they did stay at his apartment, he somehow knew how to stay in his place. He didn't believe in disciplining children that wasn't his, he always let Andrea handle that. He thought she did a great job as a mother—he never intervened with her parenting. He assisted her as she gathered the trash from the table, grabbed her bags and purse, then they were all on their way to the arcade.

A few hours later, Marcus returned home from the mall with his ready-made family, noticing as soon as he turned into the parking lot, an orange '64 Chevy Impala when it got behind him. He recognized the car immediately as belonging to someone he knew, but he didn't understand why he was being paid a visit, "Baby, take the girls inside and I'll be in there in a few minutes," he said after he parked.

"Why, what are you about to do?" Andrea asked.

"Just do as you're told. Go in there and wait for me."

He stayed put and watched in his rearview mirror as Andrea took the girls inside the apartment. He knew it was probable that she would peek through the living room window, so as soon as he jumped out of his Honda Accord, he went straight to the passenger side of the Chevy Impala.

"'H' up, cuzz," the driver said.

"What's up, Bullet. I hope you got a good reason for being here?"

"Damn, cuzz, it's like that?" Bullet replied. "You used to be my best friend, now you act like I'm in violation for coming to check on you. I'm trying to make sure everything is cool with you, but you're acting like you don't appreciate it."

"My bad, homie," said Marcus as they gave each other daps. "Bullet, we go too far back, cuzz, and I don't ever want you to think I don't appreciate you."

"I know you got a lot goin' on right now, that's why I'm making it my business to check on you," Bullet explained. "You've been layin' low for almost a year, so I really don't see them fuckin' with you."

"Yeah, I know," replied Marcus. "I'm not worried about that situation no more—I'm dealing with a whole new set of problems."

"Is that the shit Shafora was telling me about?"

"It can't be," Marcus replied. "I haven't even talked to Shafora, I don't think she know about the shit I'm going through. I heard she's on pussy now?"

"Yeah, man," Bullet laughed. "I was trippin' off that shit at first, but a lot of women is on pussy these days. It seems to be the thing to do, and I don't blame 'em 'cause I like it, too."

"Me, too," said Marcus.

"What's this new shit you got goin' on though?"

"To make a long story short. My brother and I got at these bad-ass twins we met at Caesars Palace. They took us to their house after partying one night and I ended up exchanging a few words with their punk-ass pops. The fool came up dead two or three days later and they think I had something to do with it. I don't know who knocked that fool off, but I swear to God I wasn't involved."

"Damn, that's some shit," said Bullet. "Some lawyer came to the 'hood to talk to Shafora the other day, talkin' bout he needed to ask her some questions about you."

"A lawyer or a detective?" asked Marcus.

"The fool said he was a lawyer, but I really don't know who that fool was."

"Did you see him, or did she tell you about it?"

"Nah, cuzz I saw that fool myself. I was standing out there when he pulled up."

"Was it a clean-shaven white dude?" Marcus asked.

"Nah, this cat was black. He was pushin' a fat-ass Navigator, too."

"Oh yeah, that's that white broad's lawyer. The dude that got killed was her husband and they're trying to pin that shit on her. He already talked to me and my brother, but I don't know why he would want to talk to Shafora. I don't even know how he knows about her."

"Well, she did talk to him, and according to her, he only asked her some basic shit."

"That bitch probably told him all kinds of shit, you know she don't give a damn about me," Marcus said.

"If you didn't do shit, then you have no reason to be worried about nothin'."

"I'm not worried," Marcus replied. "The thing is, if they don't press charges on me by the middle of next month, their year and a day will be expired and they won't be able to file them on me. If my name keeps coming up in this bullshit, it might force them to go ahead and press charges on me. This detective is already fuckin' with me, and I can't afford to have this shit in my life right now."

"Is the detective on you about this case or the home-invasion?" asked Bullet.

"Nobody is saying nothin' about the home-invasion. Not even the dude who got shot—this other shit is the only shit they're talking about. I'm at a good place in my life right now, and I really need all this bullshit to go away."

"I feel you, cuzz," said Bullet. "I already know you don't wanna be bothered, but when Shafora told me what that lawyer wanted, I had to come down here to check on you."

"I was thinking about calling her, but I have no reason to talk to her," Marcus said.

"Do you want me to tell her something?"

"Hell nah," replied Marcus. "Don't even tell that bitch you talked to me."

"Alright, cuzz. You good—you need anything?"

"Nah man, I'm alright," Marcus smiled. "I appreciate the offer though, but you know I still got a lil' hustle about myself."

"All Hoovers do," Bullet replied.

"It's good to see you again, but I'ma let you go ahead and push out."

"Alright, groov," said Bullet as Marcus climbed out of the car and walked toward his apartment.

CHAPTER 11

Nearly four months after her husband was killed, Paige Goldwyn hung out with her new best friends as she finally prepared to go to trial, "Tangie, I don't care what anyone else says about you, you have a real talent when it comes to cutting hair," she said as she stood in the mirror. "What do you think, Chrissy? Do you like how it looks?"

"I think you're beautiful, Paige. With your hair being short like that, it reminds me of the day you walked in here," Chrissy said with admiration.

Paige smiled at Chrissy's remark and struck a pose, seemingly flattering herself, "If she can do this with a razor blade, imagine what she would be able to do if she had some scissors?"

"You would be amazed how many people discover their talent while sitting in jail," said Chrissy.

Paige was really impressed with her new haircut so she turned to her friend hoping to encourage her, "Tangie, instead of going out and committing robberies, you should really look into becoming a barber whenever you see the streets again."

"Thank you, and I'm glad you like it," Tangie said with a smile. "I'm not really this good, your good looks is what makes it look so perfect. Hopefully you don't take offense to that."

"Tangie, everyone in here knows your sexual orientation. However, I don't think of that when I look at you," Paige said in an assuring voice. "Not once have you come on to me like that, and I assume it's because you have respect for me. I look at you as a friend, Tangie, so whatever you decide to say to me, I know you're saying it out of respect."

"Well, as a friend, let me say this to you," Tangie replied. "If a woman with your looks can go in there and pick the right jury tomorrow, your looks alone is your ticket to freedom."

"And that's the god's honest truth," Chrissy agreed.

"I thank you both for the compliment and I will be sure to keep that in mind. You do know that I had some work done, right?" Paige asked as she primped her hair.

"We know, but it looks natural," said Chrissy.

"And, it looks good," Tangie quickly added.

"Look at you with all the steatopygia you got back there. I hear men really like that?" Paige said with a smirk.

"Steato, who?" asked Tangie.

"Steatopygia. It's a medical term my husband used to use all the time. It only means that you have a lot of ass," Paige explained as they all laughed.

"Speaking of ass. Since you haven't slept with that detective yet, maybe you should let him see what yours tastes like," Tangie suggested.

"Other than shit, what else could it taste like?" said Paige, regretting telling her friend about her personal business.

"Yours might be a little sweeter than that—let him tell you after he does it," Tangie joked, quickly realizing it was time to change the subject. "And, just for the record, I can't really speak for men, but I can say for certain that women really appreciate what I have to offer."

Before leaving the cell, the women wiped down the sink and swept the floor then headed into the dayroom where they joined a group of women who were playing cards.

Just after three o'clock that afternoon, Paige was elated when she was called for an attorney visit—something she had been looking forward to the entire day. When she arrived upstairs, her attorney Donald Brown was pacing back and forth inside the small room, staring at the floor with his hands in his pockets, acting as if something was really eating away at him, "Hey gorgeous, I hope you're ready for your big day," he said as soon as she entered.

"I thought I was, but I'm not so sure now after seeing that look of uncertainty you have on your face," she said as she shook his hand. "I know it's Sunday, but I was hoping you would come down to see me today. Hopefully you're ready to kick some ass tomorrow."

"I am. I mean, it's not going to be easy, but I'm ready to see what kind of challenge they pose," he said as he crossed his legs. "The judge denied all of our pretrial motions, which doesn't really matter since they only have circumstantial evidence to begin with."

"Without any real evidence, it shouldn't be hard for us to win this case," Paige said, hoping her attorney would agree.

"It's definitely going to be interesting," he quickly replied. "I don't think that I've ever had a case like this."

"Is that good or bad?"

"I don't know yet. I'm really not sure what they're up to."

The thought flashed in her mind about what the detective had told her, so she paused for a moment before asking her next question, "You do have a plan, right?"

"Of course I do. I just can't say which way I'll go until the district attorney lays his cards on the table," he said with a sigh. "Paige, I'm going to level with you. Even though I have a perfect trial record, I have never defended a white client who was being accused of killing a black person. That may or may not present a problem for me."

"What difference does it make what color I am?"

"Oh, it makes a big difference," he replied. "In some cases it makes all the difference in the world, including life or death."

"It just doesn't seem fair to me," she said as she shook her head. "Detective Bruno pretty much said the same thing. He said we should pick as many white men for the jury as possible. He also said that I should have hired a white attorney to represent me."

"I never did like that guy or what he stands for. Everything about him is disgusting to me," he said sternly. "If I were you, I wouldn't believe anything a coward like that has to say. I'm your attorney, and it's solely my responsibility to come up with a strategy that works best for you."

"Well, he has to at least know a little something about what he's talking about. He told me the jury we pick will make the difference in this case, now you're pretty much telling me the same thing. Are you saying that white men should not be picked for my jury?"

"Well, Paige, that's the million dollar question. It could go either way. It all depends on how you're looking at it," he said as he leaned back in his chair. "Detective Bruno is looking at it his way, I'm looking at it my way, and I'm sure the district attorney has his own way of looking at it, too. There are many ways to look at this, but the person who analyzes it best, will probably be the one who'll win the case."

"And how are you looking at it?" Paige asked, really wanting to know.

"I'm looking at it from all angles. I'm basically using my personal experiences from previous juries trying to figure out who would be best for yours," he said as he loosened his tie. "Sometimes I try to look at things from an outside perspective. If I can view it the way an outsider would, it'll help me think like an outsider."

"It makes sense," said Paige, not really understanding what he was getting at.

"This case makes it more difficult to do," he said.

Sensing her attorney was not being straight with her, Paige felt herself getting upset and she wanted to know what he was hiding from her, "Why is this case so different from any other case?"

"Because it's impossible to tell what people are thinking. I'm a black man representing a white woman who the district attorney will say killed her black husband," he said slowly. "That's not an easy one to figure out."

"I'm paying you good money to figure it out," she snapped. "I'm not just paying you to represent me, Mr. Brown. I'm paying you to get me out of here!"

"And that's exactly what I hope to do," said her attorney.

Without wavering, Paige was clearly upset when she hit the tabletop with her fist and spoke her mind, "Then stop playing this guessing game with me and lets figure out exactly who would be best for my jury."

"Okay, here's what I'm thinking," he said suddenly. "I think the majority of black people would almost automatically sympathize with other blacks who are victimized by white people. Especially in certain situations," he leaned forward. "Normally, black women would probably sympathize with a black man who has been killed, but in this case, they're more likely to be less sympathetic with James because he was a successful black doctor who married a white woman instead of a black one. I think they would be the ones to pick for your jury," he said before pausing. "On the other hand, we definitely have to keep black men off the jury because they have it in their minds that white women are known for setting up black men, especially in court," he continued. "White men may look at you as a disgrace, because as beautiful as you are, you chose to marry a black man instead of one of them. They may feel betrayed by you."

"I'm well-traveled, Mr. Brown. I've seen interracial couples of all types all over the world and it's not shunned upon like it used to be. You see it everywhere you go and everybody is doing it," she explained.

"I totally agree," he said while nodding. "Las Vegas is a melting pot of different nationalities and different cultures, however, race plays a big part when it comes to the courtroom."

"What about white women, would they be good for the jury?"

"Now, that's a tricky one," he said before clearing his throat. "In my opinion, white women are a lot more open-minded than white men. A white woman might be more inclined to give you a chance just because you're one of them. On the other hand, they might see you as an outcast. Since you can't look at a person and tell if they've been brainwashed or not, we would be taking a huge risk if we chose white women to sit on your jury, and we can't afford to take those kind of risks."

"You have a tough job ahead of you," she said softly.

"My job is to save your life, and I would be really uncomfortable putting someone on the jury that I'm uncertain about. Like I said, the person who analyzes this the best, will be the person who will more than likely win the case. Not to mention, there are some really good men and women out there, black and white, who could care less about the nationality of other people. Just some honest, non-racist people who would only pay attention to the facts in the case," he said, not wanting to offend her. "Right now, I'm just juggling thoughts and ideas around in my head, but I'll have it all figured out by tomorrow morning."

"It sounds like a game," she said sadly.

"It is a game," he replied. "Going to trial is a huge gamble. Only in this game, the stakes are higher. Much higher. Instead of risking your money—you're risking your life. Fortunately for you though, you were able to afford to hire a good attorney. Not everyone can say that, and a lot of people are on death row or serving life sentences, not because they're guilty, but because they didn't have the money to hire a lawyer."

Immediately, Paige thought about the women inside her module who were always complaining about their public defenders, "It's sad."

"It is, because it basically comes down to who performs the best. If I put on the best performance, you'll go home, but if the DA does, you'll go to prison. I'm not saying it's fair, I'm just being honest about it."

"That's scary," she said, feeling more nervous than ever before. "What do you think the outcome will be?"

"There's no way to know until it happens. I will do everything I can to get you home, though."

"I hope so, because I miss everything about being at home. My privacy, wearing my own clothes, my feminine hygiene products. I miss my bidet," she said with a grin.

Knowing she was serious, he tried but couldn't hold back his smile, "A lot of women doesn't even know what that is. That's just more proof that shows you've lived a pampered life. Let's hope that we can get you back to it."

"What are they saying they have against me?" she asked with a concerned look.

"I've been going over the discovery forwards and backwards, and there's nothing in it that worries me. What worries me is that a case like this is even going to trial. They haven't even offered a plea bargain. It just doesn't seem right, but we'll see what happens once trial begins."

"Let's hope for the best," she said.

"That's all we can do."

After the enlightening visit she had with her attorney, Paige Goldwyn was completely shaken as she descended the steps, feeling more vulnerable than ever—wondering what the next day had in store for her.

CHAPTER 12

At nine o'clock Monday morning, Judge Miyasato's courtroom quickly filled with potential jurors as Paige Goldwyn sat nervously next to her attorney, "I can't believe I'm in this situation," she said, shaking. "This is the kind of stuff you see on TV."

"I know, I live for these kind of moments," her attorney replied. "Try to be as calm as possible in front of these people because you never know which ones will end up as jurors. And, try not to let Burch see how nervous you are because he'll feed off of it and use it as fuel."

A few feet from where they sat, Prosecutor Ricardo Burch didn't appear to have a care in the world. He used his index finger to browse through his notes, carefully highlighting the parts he felt was important. Occasionally, he would glance over at the defendant's table. He had nothing personal against Paige Goldwyn, but her attorney Donald Brown was a different story. The defense attorney had beat him terribly the last time he faced him in court, but this time he hoped the results would be different. He had a personal vendetta against the man. No one from the district attorney's office had ever beat

Mr. Brown in court, and he hoped to be the first to claim victory.

Once the entire courtroom had taken their seats, Bailiff Willie Clayton, who appeared to be fresh out of the military, walked stiffly up the aisle eyeing everyone closely before standing by the door where the judge would enter. His uniform was immaculate. Heavily starched and creased down to the bone, one could easily tell that the man meant business, "All rise!" he shouted as Judge Yen Miyasato entered the courtroom.

Through radiant blue eyes, Paige turned around to look at her daughters—hoping to reassure them that everything would be fine. They sat side-by-side on the courtroom's front row, accompanied by Meagan and Alix who had shut down the parlor for the rest of the week so they could be there to offer emotional support.

"This is the matter of Paige Goldwyn versus the State of Nevada," he said as he put on his glasses. "Mrs. Goldwyn starts trial today for first-degree murder, and I take it both parties are ready to proceed?"

"That's correct, Your Honor," both attorneys conceded.

"Alrighty then," the judge said.

Once he carefully explained the process to the entire jury pool, each of the potential jurors were questioned one-by-one by both attorneys. Shortly thereafter, the grueling process began to eliminate the ones they felt were not best-suited to serve as jurors.

Six hours later, all one hundred and forty potential jurors had been questioned, and after both sides used up their peremptory challenges, twelve jurors and two alternates remained in the jury box. Paige sat at the defense table, carefully scanning their faces before tapping her attorney's leg—giving her sign of approval. The jury consisted of eight women and four men, with six of the women being African-American. Although it was ultimately the jury she and her attorney had wanted, there was someone lurking inside the courtroom who had to remain quiet as he strongly opposed. As Judge Miyasato began swearing in the jurors, Detective Frank Bruno, who was wearing a partial disguise, quickly stood from his seat and made his exit. With only two white men being picked as jurors, he concluded in his own mind that Paige's chances of winning were slim to none.

Jury selection had taken the entire day, and because of this, Judge Yen Miyasato adjourned the court and scheduled opening statements to begin at nine AM the following morning.

Later that evening, Paige could not stop herself from smiling as she discussed jury selection with Tangie and Chrissy. Going into intricate detail to explain the proceedings, she didn't notice other women were listening closely before she was called upstairs for a legal visit. Normally when she got a visit, every time she reached the top of the steps there would always be an officer there waiting for her. This time was different. An overweight officer was working the visiting post, and instead of leaving her chair more than necessary—she found it to be a lot easier to just sit at the control panel and click the doors.

"Your visitor is in room four," she said before taking a sip of her diet soda. "Whenever you're done just press the call-button and I'll pop you out."

"Okay," Paige replied.

Feeling like she had a solid chance of winning her case, Paige suddenly found it hard to conceal her emotions as she raced toward the door when she heard it click. As soon as she pushed it open, her anticipation of seeing her attorney quickly faded away when she saw Detective Bruno sitting there, "Oh, hi Frank," she said as the door closed behind her. "I wasn't expecting to see you here."

Before she could sit down, Detective Bruno was already up on his feet yelling at her, "Why did you hire that idiot attorney? Do you have any idea how screwed you are?"

Confused by his anger, she hesitated a moment before replying, "What's wrong, did I miss something?"

"Did you miss something? Sweetheart, it would be a miracle if you don't miss out on the rest of your life," he said while turning red. "What the hell was he thinking picking all of those niggers to sit on your jury? Those people won't help you!"

"Frank, why is it always about race with you?" she shot back, surprised to hear him speak so openly.

"Sweetie, you have no clue how serious this is, do you? This isn't a case about race, it's about justice, and I don't see a jury like that having sympathy for you. Especially since one of their own was put in the ground," he stated bluntly. "Are you sure your attorney is trying to help you? What the hell was he thinking striking all of those good white men from the jury pool just so he could put those spooks in the jury box? White people were your only hope. They're the ones who would have been more than likely to give you an acquittal."

Tired of his racist remarks, she looked directly at him and kindly spoke, "Frank, do you honestly believe that shit, or are you just saying that because that's what you'd do?"

"A jury of your peers is what you need, Paige, but your idiot attorney just blew it for you!" he replied. "What made you hire him out of all the good attorneys you had at your disposal?"

"There may have been some good ones, Frank, but how many do you know besides Donald Brown who can honestly say they've never lost a case?"

He thought for a moment before replying, "I can't say for certain."

"That's what I thought. As loosely as you keep using the term idiot, you can't name anyone, not even a white attorney who can infatically say they've never lost a case. If anything, they would love to be idiots too, if being an idiot means they're one of the best."

Clearly frustrated, the detective leaned back in his chair, tapping his foot on the floor before replying, "He just got lucky. Just like he was lucky enough to escape the ghetto, but I still wouldn't have hired him to represent me."

"Frank, I'm the one on trial here, not you. If I'm found guilty, I'm the one who'll go to prison, not you! I picked him because I wanted the best to represent me. With that being said, I have to at least give him the chance to prove that he knows what he's doing," she replied angrily. "If I'm willing to give him that chance, I think you should be willing to do the same."

"Okay," he said, throwing his hands in the air. "If that's what you want, I'll go ahead and see what happens. I still think it was a mistake to hire him, but I'll wait and see what happens tomorrow."

"That's all I ask," she said nicely. "Why are you so concerned anyway?"

"It's not a good time to answer that, but I hope to be able to answer it soon," he replied.

Hoping to find a way to cope with her increasing fear, the thought of suicide briefly went through Paige's mind—she desperately wanted the ordeal to come to an end.

"M-80, stop being a punk, man," said BumperJack as he stood slumped over with his hands in his pockets. "You know we need you on this one, man, everybody else is too scary to help us pull it off."

"Bump, I don't do that no more, man," Marcus replied. "I still sell a lil' dope every now and then, but home invasions is a thing of the past for me."

"Andrea must got his ass on lockdown," Lil' Ray interjected. "Ever since he's been messing with her his ass has been on the straight and narrow."

"I know," BumperJack laughed. "I'm surprised he's still selling dope, he need to cut that out and start going to church."

"I already do," said Marcus. "Look, homie, don't get mad at me 'cause I've changed my life. I've done a lot of dumb shit in my life but I refuse to be dumb for the rest of my life. None of us had fathers growing up, man, and look how fucked up we turned out to be. I don't wanna see Andrea's girls turn out like us. I'm the only father they know, and I can't jeopardize them losing me."

"Alright, homie. We gon' go ahead and push out," said BumperJack. "We can't get you to roll with us, so I guess me and Lil' Ray will do it ourselves."

"Let's do this," Lil' Ray said, smiling.

"Let's make it hap'n cap'n," BumperJack added as they walked towards the door.

Marcus immediately jumped in front of the two men and peeked outside before letting them leave.

"M-80, what's up, man? Why the fuck are you acting so paranoid?" asked BumperJack.

"I'm just trying to make sure the coast is clear," Marcus replied.

"Clear, for what?" Lil' Ray asked.

"This detective has been sweatin' me lately and I've caught his ass hanging around the spot a few times."

"Sweatin' you for what?" asked BumperJack.

"About a hot-one I had nothing to do with," said Marcus. "Watch the news tonight and you'll see what I'm talking about. The dude's wife started trial today for his murder but they're still sweatin' me for some fuckin' reason."

"Did you know the dude?" Lil' Ray asked.

"Man, I met the fool one time when me and my brother went over there with his twin daughters. I had an argument with the dude and that's the only reason why they think I knocked him off."

"That don't sound right, homie," replied BumperJack. "They can't think you knocked him off if they've already arrested his wife for it."

"I know it don't make no sense, but this detective has been sweatin' me like a motherfucker. Every time I see this fool he reminds me of the motherfucker that got the homie, Mouse. And, you know they got him on some bullshit."

"I miss the homie, too, cuzz," said BumperJack. "That case was fucked up from the gate and they still gave the homie all-day for that shit. He's been down for about eighteen years now."

"Yeah, I know. That's what happens when a poor black man gets caught up in these white folks justice system. I hope the homie see daylight again, though."

"M-80, we're about to go ahead and bounce," said BumperJack. "You stay up, cuzz, and I'll let you know how it turns out."

"Alright, homie, y'all be careful," Marcus replied.

He watched the two men walk away—hoping they would change their minds before committing another act of senseless violence. BumperJack and Lil' Ray were his old acquaintances who had always accompanied him in the past when he went out to do home invasions. He had stopped participating eleven months earlier, so he was really taken aback when he returned home from Aria—CityCenter's Hotel and Casino, and they were sitting on his doorstep waiting for him. They knew he had vowed to never do robberies again and it bothered him to think they hadn't taken him seriously. As soon as the

Pathfinder sped out of the parking lot, Marcus looked around once more, before going back inside and locking the door.

CHAPTER 13

Eyes red from a lack of sleep, Amp kneeled on one knee outside of the Greyhound station when his beautiful young daughter emerged from the bus, "Come here, baby," he said in a joyous voice.

Jada ran nearly full-speed into her father's arms—the impact nearly knocked him backwards as she locked her arms tightly around his neck, "Hi, daddy," she said before collapsing her head onto his shoulder. "I miss you, daddy. Mommy and grandma told me to tell you hi."

"How is mommy?" Amp said as he kissed her cheek.

"She's doing a lot better. She asked me not to worry about her," she said with a burst of energy that showed how happy she was to see her dad.

Sitting beside the bus next to the luggage compartment, were two Louis Vuitton suitcases that belonged to Jada. Amp felt the luggage was inappropriate for an eight-year-old, and since she had traveled alone, she could have easily become a victim of theft or something worse, he thought. He was too excited to harbor such thoughts so he pushed them from his mind then stared at his daughter—not believing how much she'd grown since the last time he'd seen her, "Have you had breakfast yet?" he asked as he loaded the suitcases into the trunk of his Porsche.

"No, but I'm not really hungry," Jada replied.

Minutes later, they were sitting at a table in a restaurant in the Plaza—a hotel and casino adjacent to the Greyhound station. Over breakfast, he asked his daughter how she felt about having to move to Las Vegas from Seattle, Washington. She said she had no problem with it, but said that she would miss her friends and the school she attended. Amp had met her mom, Nikki several years back while in Seattle on business, and their messing around led to the conception of Jada. Although he and Nikki had called it quits, he had been there for his daughter since the day she was born. He flew to Washington once a month, talked to her frequently on the phone, but she had never come down to live with him. It was something he had always wanted, but was just now getting the chance to experience it.

After eating breakfast, Amp left a tip and paid the bill before guiding his daughter to the ladies bathroom. As he waited for her outside, he suddenly decided to make a call.

"What's good?" said Bull when he answered the phone.

"That's exactly what I'm calling to find out," said Amp.

"Ah, man, everything is running smooth. All the girls are currently out on calls, except for Jazmin. She's takin' the day off to handle some business, but she'll make up for it tomorrow, though," Bull said before pausing. "Did you pick Jada up from the bus station?"

"Oh yeah, we just got done eating breakfast. My baby is growing up man, and I look forward to spending some time with her."

"I assume that means you're not working today?"

"I doubt it," Amp replied. "Not until I find Jada a babysitter. I can't leave her by herself in that big ass house, and you know I can't bring her to the office with me."

"Man, go ahead and spend the day with your daughter, and work on trying to find a babysitter. I got TopNotch Entertainment under control today, but I need you to come handle business tomorrow. Something important has come up and I gotta take a trip to Cali tonight—but I should be back by tomorrow morning."

"When were you planning on telling me this?" Amp asked as Jada came from the bathroom drying her hands.

Bull thought about it before answering the question then laughed into the phone as he did so, "I just found out about it thirty minutes ago. It's no big deal, dog. It's gon' be a quick trip, I just gotta handle some important business. It shouldn't take no longer than five-six hours."

"Alright, man. We'll discuss it later. I guess you'll have to wait until tomorrow to meet my daughter," Amp said before hanging up.

He and Jada spent the entire morning together. He stopped at the mall to buy her some new outfits, took a trip to the Vegas zoo, even went to ride go-carts for a couple of hours. He couldn't get enough of seeing her laugh. And, the innocence she possessed, he knew he would do everything he could to make sure she kept it.

"Daddy, I'm sleepy, can we go home now?" she said while batting her eyes.

Amp had grown tired himself so he was more than happy to oblige. When they arrived home, he watched his daughter fall asleep on the living room couch. He then closed his eyes to take a nap himself, but recalled the conversation he had with Bull—something just didn't seem right with the man's voice. Amp tried to narrow it down, but he just couldn't put his finger on it.

It was nine-fifteen when the plane landed at the Metropolitan Oakland International Airport. Bull made his exit, feeling the slight breeze of the cool California air as he hoisted his bag over his shoulder and headed toward the terminal. He was uncomfortable carrying the amount of cash he had in his bag, but he was only in town to handle some business, so his eyes were immediately in search of the person he'd come to see. Lonnie Garner had promised to be there waiting for him as soon as he exited the plane but, so far, things weren't going according to plan. *I hope everything go smooth,* he said to himself. Bull looked around aimlessly as he walked through the airport and was reaching for his cell phone when a woman approached him.

"Are you here for Lonnie?" she said with a spanish accent.

"Yes, I am. Who are you?"

"I'm his wife Claudia, he sent me here to pick you up."

"Oh, hi Claudia. I'm Bull," he said as he shook her hand.

"How do you do?"

"I'm fine now," Bull replied. "I knew he said he would be here waiting for me, and I was beginning to get nervous when I didn't see him."

Claudia smiled, "No need to worry, you're in good hands now."

"I see," Bull said under his breath. He followed closely behind Claudia as she led him to the front of the terminal where she'd parked her car right next to the curb. He had only met Lonnie Garner in person a couple of times, and from what he'd seen so far—he could tell that the man had exquisite taste.

"Is your bag okay, or would you like for me to put it in my trunk for you?" Claudia said as she turned to him.

"I think the trunk would be good," Bull replied. He found himself very attracted to Claudia, but he knew she was probably out of his league.

"How'd you get a name like Bull?" said Claudia as she pulled down the trunk of her Infiniti.

"I don't know," said Bull. "Some people say it's because of my build, but others have said it's because of my strength."

"That's plausible, I think it's a moniker that suits you," she said as they climbed in the car.

Bull was confused. He didn't know whether or not Claudia had insulted him or given him a compliment so he made it his business to clarify it, "Is that a good or bad thing?"

"Being a powerful man is never a bad thing."

Is she flirting with me, he wondered? *I could have swore her eyes twinkled when she looked at me.* Bull knew his mind was probably playing tricks on him. He'd had it happen to him before on previous occasions. As they sped away from the terminal, Bull's thoughts continued to race out of control. He visualized Claudia's golden brown skin, her long black hair, and her small petite body lying next to him. He wondered what she looked like naked—everything about her was delicious to him and, he assumed she probably taste as good as she looked, "How far is Lonnie from here?"

"We live close to Lake Merritt—about an hour away," she said.

"I like your accent, are you from here?"

"No, I'm from Colombia," she smiled. "I met Lonnie in my country and he brought me here nearly ten years ago."

"I'm surprised you haven't lost your accent yet. But that's a good thing, because it's sexy as hell."

Claudia smiled as she glanced at him, but her attention was immediately back on the road, "Is it possible that Bull could be short for bullshit?"

He laughed at her sarcasm, but didn't miss the opportunity to get his point across, "I'm serious. I think you're sexy as hell and I'm jealous of Lonnie for finding you first."

"I've always been a sucker for compliments, so you better be careful what you say to me."

"I stand by my word," replied Bull. He was suddenly at a loss for words, but his thoughts continued to run rapidly.

They rode in silence from that point on until Claudia pulled inside a gated-community, "This is home," she said with innocence—the streetlight accentuating her exotic features.

Bull was impressed with the upperclass neighborhood. He looked around, taking in as much as he could. Unlike the Southern Highlands Community he lived in, everything in this neighborhood was high-end. He didn't think living could get any better than he already lived, but when Claudia pulled her Infiniti into the circular driveway—parking behind a Bently—Bull knew that he had to step his game up. He and Claudia walked toward the mansion after removing his bag from the trunk, and they was greeted at the door by her smiling husband, "Hi Sweetie, I see you found my friend here?" he said to Claudia while approaching Bull, extending his hand. "Good to see you my friend. I'm glad to see you had a safe trip."

"Thank you. It's good to see you, too, Lonnie," Bull said after releasing his grip.

"Come into my home and let's do business," he said while gesturing with his hand, wanting Bull to walk in front of him.

Bull walked inside, admiring the marble floor and matching pillars. He stopped in the middle of the floor and placed his hands on his hips, absorbing everything he saw—expensive statues, Picasso and Rembrandt paintings—he knew he was in the company of a man who had very expensive taste—surpassing his own, "I wanna be just like you when I grow up, Lonnie," he smiled. "This is what it means to live large, huh?"

"This is what happens when you're on top of your game," Lonnie replied, exalted to see Bull was impressed. "Honey, go fetch this man a drink. I want to get this done as soon as possible, I have other things that I need to do tonight."

Bull watched as Claudia followed instructions and went to the bar, but not before she'd rolled her eyes at her husband. She came back immediately carrying two drinks, and Bull naturally assumed that they were for he and Lonnie. He took his drink as she handed it to him and was surprised when she downed the other shot herself. He sensed that she and Lonnie were not that happy together, and he began making plans to capitalize on it. He reached for his bag after gulping his drink, poured the large amount of money onto the table, then looked squarely at Lonnie before chanting, "Let's do business."

"Atta boy," replied Lonnie. "Let's get this done so we can get you back to the airport."

Bull was happy after completing the transaction. He even tested a sample, so he knew that he had a high-quality product.

"Bull, it was a pleasure doing business with you, I hope it's not long before we do it again."

"Dido, Lonnie. I'm sure we'll be seeing each other again soon," Bull said, instantly remembering the conversation between he and Amp.

"Honey, take this man back to the airport. We don't want him to miss his plane," Lonnie said to Claudia. "I have other endeavors that needs my attention, so I'll see you later when I get back home."

"Okay," she said as she kissed him on the cheek.

Bull was up on his feet and ready to go when Lonnie rushed out the house, leaving him alone with Claudia, "Damn, is he always like that?"

"What do you mean?" said Claudia.

"The guy's a jerk—I think he should treat you with more respect."

"That's Lonnie," Claudia replied. "He wasn't like that when we met ten years ago—I think his wealth has given him a big head."

"I think so, too," Bull agreed. "There are not many women in this world as beautiful as you. He should be going out of his way to treat you special."

"Bull, you shouldn't say things like that. I told you that I'm a sucker for compliments," she blushed. "Would you like another drink before we go back to the airport?"

"That would be cool. My plane doesn't leave for another two hours."

Bull was beginning to feel sorry for Claudia. He had heard stories about wealthy Americans going over to other countries bringing women back to the United States, just to use them as slaves, but he wasn't sure if that's what he'd stumbled upon. He didn't know the depth of Lonnie and Claudia's relationship, or of their unhappiness—but he was of the opinion—she deserved better. He tossed back another shot of the expensive liquor as he sat at the bar—really beginning to resent Lonnie as he stared at Claudia, so he pulled her between his legs and held her close. She reciprocated his advances by wrapping her arms around him, covering his mouth with hers before sticking her tongue deeply down his throat. She guided him to a different section of the house where they stripped down naked, and were all over each other in record time. What they didn't know was, her husband forgot his cell phone on top of the pillar, and was heading back home to retrieve it.

CHAPTER 14

Tuesday afternoon during lunch recess, Paige and her attorney sat facing each other in a deliberating room just a few feet away from the judge's chamber. They had just wrapped up two and a half hours of opening statements and there were tears streaming down both sides of her face when the district attorney finished his second statement, "What was that all about, and why didn't we get to argue twice?" she asked while dabbing the wetness from her eyes. "Those things are not true what he said about me."

"Paige, everything that just happened is part of the process," her attorney explained. "The same thing that just happened during opening statements will all happen again during closing arguments. That's just how the rules of law are written."

"How is that fair, though?" she asked.

"Since the state has the burden of proving its case against you, the district attorney gets to argue twice—leaving us with only one shot to prove our case. That's the protocol of jury trials but it doesn't mean that we should just throw in the towel," he said as he leaned back.

"It just seems so unfair to me," she replied. "Don't get me wrong. I think you gave a damn good argument, but by the time he finished his second argument, the jury probably forgot everything you said."

"That's why they're up there taking notes," he stated solemnly. "They're writing down everything that they think is relevant, and when the time comes for them to make a decision, they'll refer to their notes and recall everything that was said on both sides."

"I don't think I can take anymore of this. It's not cool. I mean, my life is in jeopardy, and I'm supposed to just sit there without saying anything and expect that the jury will do the right thing? This is ridiculous."

"Paige, you don't have to trust them, but I do need you to trust me," he said while rubbing her hand. "I have a lot of experience at this, and I know what I'm doing, okay? I've already explained to the jury that this case was built on circumstantial evidence, and if they didn't catch it then, they will once the district attorney starts presenting his case," he said. "It's my job to make sure he doesn't say anything that he can't prove, and if he does, I'm going to pick him apart piece by piece," he continued in an assuring voice. "I want him to make that mistake, because the more pieces I can prove doesn't fit anywhere, the weaker and weaker their case becomes," he said, issuing a half-hearted smile. "Just believe me when I tell you that I know what I'm doing. If I don't tell you to worry—that means you have nothing to worry about."

"He called me beauty and the beast, and told the jury to overlook my beauty and see me as the beast that I really am," said Paige.

"He wants a conviction. Mr. Burch is considered to be one of the best prosecutors in the State of Nevada. He's been known to cry in front of the jury and everything else. There were rumors several years ago that he paid a witness a few thousand dollars just to come to court to give false testimony. Something they've never been able to prove," he quickly added. "The man is an actor but so am I. Once this trial is over with, maybe he'll wish he was in Hollywood somewhere instead of wasting so much of his time in the DA's office."

Paige smiled a little but her nervousness was still very apparent, "Does he have a good record of getting convictions?"

"The majority of people on death row or serving life sentences in the State of Nevada is where they are because of him," he said in a more serious tone. "This short old man is probably in his mid sixties and he uses it to his advantage every chance he gets. He has a reputation of literally falling to his knees in front of the jury and has threatened to pack his bags and leave the state if they didn't come back with a guilty verdict."

"He sounds like an asshole, and I don't like him," said Paige.

"Join the club, sweetheart. Join the club," her attorney said as he glanced at his watch. "Well, we better get back inside if we don't want the judge getting mad at us."

Three days later, after hearing testimony from Detective Frank Bruno, 911 Dispatcher Charlene Moon, the coroner, an expert witness, and four uni-formed officers, the prosecution announced he rest his case. When it came time for Attorney Donald Brown to present Paige's defense, Judge Miyasato called a recess and they were put on hold until Monday morning.

CHAPTER 15

Early Saturday morning, Defense Attorney Donald Brown sat by the pond at Blue Diamond Park with a large bag of popcorn feeding the ducks. Paige Goldwyn's trial had already begun and he still wasn't sure how he was going to proceed. He was very aware that the DA's office held a grudge against him and he couldn't be sure what they had up their sleeve. He'd beaten them every time he'd taken a case to trial, and if the tables were turned, he knew that he would probably feel the same way about them as they felt about him. He remembers on a few occasions when his office and home had been burglarized—seemingly his case files were the burglars only target and he suspected the DA's office of being responsible for it. He recall times when the gas tank on his car had been tampered with. He could never seem to catch the perpetrator in the act, but the one thing he could be certain about, was that someone was trying to bring harm to him.

In the past, he often found himself sitting in front of this same pond in the same spot on the bench while trying to figure out a way to perforate the

DA's case. This park was where he found solace when he was faced with difficulty, and as odd as it sounds, watching how the ducks interacted with one another was one of the ways that he came up with his courtroom strategies.

As birds chirped in the trees surrounding the pond, they seemed to be much more happier than the large group of ducks that had gathered around him. The majority of the ducks were watching him, fighting each other for a better position—waiting for him to throw some more popcorn, as if it was his duty to make sure they ate. That seemed to be the difference between the ducks and the birds. The ducks had been domesticated—depending on human beings to provide them with food, unlike the wild birds, who depended on themselves—maybe that was the reason they were singing with so much joy?

After throwing a handful of popcorn out to the ducks, the defense attorney watched as they fought and climbed all over each other, not caring if they hurt one another in the process. He wondered how a wild animal, who once depended on itself, had been tricked into not depending on itself anymore, but to start depending on human beings instead. The scene reminded him of something his dad used to tell him when he was eight years old.

"Son, always be responsible for yourself," his dad would say. *"I'm raising you to be a responsible young man and don't you ever allow yourself to depend on anyone other than yourself. You become helpless when you start depending on others."*

And, that's exactly how the ducks appeared to be. Helpless. He wondered what they would do if he got up and left with his bag of popcorn? How could this happen, he asked himself? He knew that he already knew the answer, and it saddened him to see that they were mentally broken. The same thing that happened to the ducks had been done to his own people in the days of slavery. His mother and father had always stressed to him how important it was for him to stand up for himself, *"Stay strong, be a man. That's what God put you on this earth to be,"* they'd say. A lot of things he was taught as a child he didn't really understand until he got older. That's when he started realizing the significance of the things he was taught and how fortunate he was to have had parents like his. Growing up in Jackson, Mississippi, all of the guys that he grew up with were either dead or tangled up on the wrong side of the law. He was the only one who had actually made it and to know what it was like to be successful. His parents instilled in him the importance of education and it turned out to be his key to success. He had watched several of his friends go from depending on their mothers to depending on their girlfriends, to depending on God and everyone else. They went from one person to another, but never once attempted to depend on themselves. And, they still had the audacity to call themselves men.

"A man's responsibility is to protect and provide for his entire household," his mom would say. *"If he doesn't know how he'll do it, it's his job to figure it out because everyone in the household is depending on him. He's supposed to make a way out of no way. That's his job as a man."*

He wondered how some of his friends could call themselves men, or if they even knew the definition of what it took to be a man? They couldn't seem to figure out how to provide for themselves, let alone an entire family, so how could they call themselves men? He wondered.

For the defense attorney, sitting there feeding the ducks had brought back some important memories. He remembers when his dad used to drive him all over Jackson, Mississippi—pointing out different apartment complexes known as the projects.

"Do you know why they're referred to as the projects?" his dad would ask.

"No," he would say in his small voice.

"The real reason they're called the projects is because they were a project," he'd say. *"The projects was a scientific project—where white folks used to experiment with black folks, trying to learn how to keep us mentally enslaved when we were no longer physically enslaved."*

It made too much sense to the defense attorney. He sat there watching the ducks—big and small, trying to see which one was in charge, but they all seemed to be only out for themselves. They had no idea how much they could achieve if they acted as a group. They all seemed to be divided—which is what made it easier for them to be mentally broken. It's the same way blacks were mentally broken in the days of slavery. The rule was to divide and conquer, so as long as they were kept separated and against each other, they would never be able to accomplish anything as a group, not realizing that they were strength in numbers.

Noticing the similarities between the ducks and his own people, the attorney felt himself getting upset so he stood from the bench, tossed the rest of the popcorn on the ground in front of the ducks, then heard them fighting each other as he walked off.

Later that evening, as Michelle's warm soft hands massaged his masculine shoulders, he became so relaxed that he almost forgot the business at hand.

"How does that feel?" Michelle asked in a seductive voice.

"Ooh, it's too good to describe," said the defense attorney without opening his eyes.

"Good. Maybe it'll help you be at your best when trial resumes Monday morning. You know we're counting on you to bring our mom back home."

"That's right," Melissa added as her hands worked hard to loosen his calves.

"Well, that's exactly what I hope to do," the attorney said as his eyes opened, "I need to go over what happened with you two again. It should only take a minute, but since I'll be calling you both to testify Monday morning, I need to go over the facts one more time just to make sure everything is set and ready to go," he explained. "Michelle, if you don't mind, run it by me verbatim everything that was said when you two arrived home that Saturday morning."

As they continued to give him a dual massage, both Michelle and Melissa took turns explaining exactly what happened two days before their dad was killed. The attorney already knew the case forwards and backwards, so instead of writing down any additional notes, he just compared them to the facts he already had in his mind, "Melissa, the last time we spoke, you said that you and Rashad were sort of dating?"

"Not anymore," Melissa replied. "I broke up with him over a week ago—we haven't spoken or anything at all since then."

"What happened?" the attorney asked, expressing interest.

"I just didn't want anything else to do with him," Melissa said as she glanced at Michelle.

"When the two of you were dating, did you ever have any discussions with him or his brother about their possible involvement in your father's death?"

"No!" she said with an attitude. "Marcus and I were never around each other, and Rashad and I had an agreement never to bring up the subject."

"How was it possible to be around each other without bringing it up?" he asked while looking at her. "I mean, with your life being impacted the way it has, how could you have possibly avoided not bringing it up?"

"Easy," she said while shrugging her shoulders. "It became a dead issue once we agreed not to talk about it."

Uncertain how to respond, Defense Attorney Donald Brown yawned and stretched his arms before rolling onto his side to sit upright, "Well, I think that covers everything for now," he said as he yawned again. "I thank you both for the wonderful massage, and I don't think I'll be forgetting about it any time soon. If I think of anything else before Monday morning, I know how to get in touch with you."

"Okay," Michelle replied. "Don't forget we're counting on you to bring her back to us."

"I'll do everything I can—I promise you."

After getting dressed, Attorney Donald Brown removed his wallet from his back pocket and gave a hefty tip before leaving the parlor. He had been practicing law for seventeen years, had done hundreds of interviews, and not once had he ever experienced anything like this. Being massaged at once by the beautiful twins was so exhilarating—he wanted more than ever to bring their mom back home. He climbed behind the wheel of his Navigator, realized how hungry he was, so he stopped at a Chinese restaurant not far from his home. As he sat tucked in a corner of the small restaurant, his mind once again returned to Michelle and Melissa, recalling the softness of their hands as they rubbed his body. Before he knew it, the beautiful evening had turned into night, and he smiled to himself because he knew he would never forget such a pleasant experience.

Thick somberness hovered over the large living room—everyone was sad and visibly shaken, the only sounds in the air was sniveling and sobbing. Amp lay hunched over in the deep-seated couch, almost curled in a fetal position as Chyna consoled him, simultaneously wiping her own eyes while stroking him gently across his back. Kim, Jazmin, Amanda and Missy had all collapsed in various parts of the living room, weeping uncontrollably, trying hard to make sense of what had happened. Veronica, who had become sick to her stomach, could be heard coughing and violently spewing up vomit as she stood over the toilet in a nearby bathroom. No one said much to each other. They were all at a loss for words as they struggled to cope with the terrible tragedy. Bull had been brutally murdered in California the night before. His new ecstasy connection, Lonnie Garner, had caught him having sex with his wife in the basement of their home, less than an hour after selling him a large quantity of ecstasy. To see Bull thrusting between his wife's legs must have filled the man with uncontrollable rage—because he ran a sword through both of their bodies—leaving them both pinned tightly together, which is how they were when the police arrived. Lonnie Garner never left the scene and was taken into custody for two counts of murder.

Amp had to send Jada to live with Chyna's mother for a few days while he tried to come to grips with what had happened. Bull had been a great friend and business partner and the memories they shared would never be forgotten. Amp knew he was going to miss him terribly. They vowed to always remain loyal to one another—and with so many secrets between the two of them, now that Bull was gone, Amp was undecided about what he'd do. He only remembers feeling like this one other time in his life and that's when he'd gotten the news that Michael Jackson had died. He and Bull were both big fans of the King of Pop, and now that they were both gone, things were even more difficult.

CHAPTER 16

It was just past eight AM Sunday morning. Marcus stood shirtless in front of the stove trying to prepare breakfast for he and his girlfriend. It was not something he was accustomed to doing, but since he and Andrea had just finished smoking a blunt, it wasn't hard for her to talk him into it.

As he tried his best to concentrate, his eyes kept shooting in Andrea's direction as she sat on the edge of the living room couch wearing black see-through panties and a gray sports bra—focused strictly on sealing the blunt she'd rolled. He watched as she licked it from one end to the other before twirling it continuously between her fingers then laid on her back and looked at him.

"Baby, hurry up so we can blaze this up," she said in a raspy voice.

"Girl, we need to eat something before we fuck with that," he replied while scraping the eggs from the bottom of the skillet. "I'm having a hard time staying focused now, so let me come down a little before we smoke some more."

UNFAIR

Andrea smiled and spread her legs apart before pressing the blunt against her recently-shaved pussy, "We've only smoked one. Since you like tasting my kitty-kat so much, maybe you'll smoke it with me if I get it wet and sticky the way you like it."

"Baby, please don't put that there," Marcus begged while approaching her. "Close your legs before my brother comes downstairs and see you doing that."

"Let's smoke one more," she pleaded.

"No!" he said sternly. "Go in there and put some clothes on and come eat these eggs since you're the one who asked me to cook this shit."

After hesitating for a few seconds, Andrea rolled her eyes as she stood from the couch and went into the bedroom to put on some clothes.

Moments later, she returned wearing some black spandex pants with a white pullover shirt that clearly exposed her erect nipples.

"Damn, you must be feeling freaky or something?" he asked as she headed toward the kitchen table.

"No, why you say that?"

"Your nipples look hard—they're as big as gumdrops."

Andrea smiled as she looked at her nipples, "Don't hate. I just got some nice ass titties."

"That's why I fuck with you," he smiled.

As soon as she and Marcus sat down to eat, Rashad came down the stairs and asked for a plate.

"Man, I can put some on a saucer for you," Marcus said as he shoved a fork-full inside his mouth.

After accepting his portion, Rashad turned around to go back upstairs but was forced to stop when someone banged on the door, "Damn, who is this knocking like the police?" he asked while going toward the door.

"It's probably that lawyer," said Marcus. "He called last night and said that he would be stopping by sometime this morning."

Rashad snatched the door open and almost tripped over his feet as he did so. He saw the well-dressed gentleman standing there so he proceeded to put on a fake smile, "Good morning, sir."

"Same to you, and it's good to see you again," the man said mild-manneredly.

"Come in. There's no need for you to stand out there," said Rashad.

"I hope this isn't a bad time," the man said.

"Nah, I knew you were coming, I just didn't know it would be this early," Marcus yelled from the kitchen table.

"This shouldn't take too long. I just wanted to be sure that we've dotted all the i's and crossed the t's before I put you both on the stand tomorrow or Tuesday," he explained as he sat on a footstool in front of the couch. "I know this is ground we've covered before but I need you both to reiterate exactly what happened that morning when you were briefly accosted by Dr. Goldwyn."

"Man, how many times do we have to keep going over this?" Marcus asked rudely.

"Hopefully it's the last time before you take the stand. I just need to be sure we're set to go."

As soon as Marcus began explaining what happened, Andrea, who hadn't said a word since sitting down at the kitchen table, quickly stood from her chair and went into the bedroom. She was pretending like she wasn't interested, but as soon as the door closed behind her, she quietly placed her ear against it.

Once Rashad and Marcus finished repeating their stories, attorney Donald Brown began prepping his most crucial witnesses on how they should conduct themselves in front of the jury. Unlike he'd felt when he first visited the apartment, after talking to the men for less than an hour, he made his exit breathing a sigh of relief—feeling he finally had what he needed to free his client. From the day he'd agreed to take the case, he could honestly say for the first time, that he didn't have any regrets about doing so.

As the weekend slowly crept to an end, Paige Goldwyn sat in front of the television, trying to prepare herself mentally for the following day. With the TV blaring throughout the module, her mind was so adrift that she didn't hear her name when she was called for a visit.

"Paige," Tangie said while tapping her leg. "You don't hear them calling you? They want you upstairs, you got a visit."

"Thanks, Tangie. I was daydreaming," Paige said with a grin.

When she got upstairs, she couldn't help but notice the masculine scent of Detective Bruno's expensive cologne. It filled the entire room and sent chills through her body that she couldn't ignore, "Good evening, Frank," she said while hugging him. "I was just thinking about you. What's the matter, you couldn't go the whole weekend without seeing me?"

"Why are you so happy this evening?" he asked while crossing his legs.

"I'm just happy to see you, that's all. I haven't seen you since you testified on Friday, and I've been wanting to thank you for your testimony."

"You don't have to thank me," he replied, smiling. "I just answered the questions that I was asked, and I must say, I was pretty impressed by the way that nig—your attorney did his job…" he said as he caught himself. "He did a decent job and gave a superb performance on cross-examination. Now all we have to do is see what happens tomorrow."

Noticing how the detective kept glancing at her breasts, Paige's juices between her legs began to flow and she desperately wanted him to scratch the itch she felt, "We're in here alone, detective, and I know that you think about me the way I think about you."

Tempted to lay her on the table and fuck her brains out, Detective Bruno slowly licked his lips while continuing to stare at her voluptuous breasts, "Sweetheart, there's too much at stake here. We have to be patient until the time is right," he said as he rose to his feet.

"Is that a hard-on you have there, detective?" Paige asked as she reached for it. "Mmm, should I bend over for you, or would you like for me to wrap my lips around it?"

He pushed her hand away and cleared his throat before pressing the call-button to leave the room.

UNFAIR

As she lay in her cell alone that night, Paige Goldwyn lie with her legs spread widely apart with her hand inside her panties, pleasuring herself. She thrust two fingers inside herself, closed her eyes and moaned softly and continued to do so until she reached orgasm. With no way of knowing, but the handsome detective she was thinking about was also in bed alone, and his only desire was to please her.

CHAPTER 17

Monday morning at the Regional Justice Center, the Honorable Judge Yen Miyasato's courtroom was packed to capacity. Paige Goldwyn sat watching her attorney intently while everyone else in the courtroom stared at the witness. A striking resemblance of her beautiful mom, Michelle Goldwyn sat fully erect on the witness-stand as she testified tearfully gazing straight at the jury. She gave the same account of events that Melissa had given, but she was twice as effective as her twin sister.

As Judge Miyasato's courtroom succumbed to silence, District Attorney Ricardo Burch appeared to be uncomfortable in his chair as he stared at Michelle on the witness-stand. In his opinion, she came across very convincingly, and he wasn't quite sure how he should handle her.

While jurors were squirming in their seats shooting glimpses at each other, Defense Attorney Donald Brown decided to take advantage of the opportunity by turning away from his witness without questioning her further.

"Would you like to cross-examine the witness, Mr. Burch?" the judge asked.

"I'm afraid not, Your Honor."

"Mr. Brown, would you call your next witness, please?" the judge asked after excusing Michelle from the witness-stand.

Without standing up, the defense attorney clasped his fingers tightly together before speaking, "Your Honor, I would like to call Marcus Myers."

When the bailiff stepped outside to call the witness, nearly everyone sitting in the crowded audience turned and stared at the door as the young black gentleman slowly entered the courtroom. He came in as if he had entered a hip-hop concert instead of a court of law—made his way toward the front of the courtroom—sporting a platinum necklace over a black hooded sweatshirt and a pair of designer jeans that was obviously too big. He strolled up the aisle cracking his knuckles while several people's eyes were fixated on him as he casually looked around dragging his feet on the floor.

"Over here, sir," the judge said while pointing toward the witness-stand.

Once he was sworn in by the bailiff, Marcus pulled up his pants and sat down and began twirling the diamond ring that he wore on his pinky.

"Good morning, sir," Attorney Donald Brown said in a soothing voice.

"Good morning," replied the witness.

"For the record, would you please state your name and spell it for us?"

"Marcus Myers. M-a-r-c-u-s M-y-e-r-s."

"Mr. Myers, do you recognize this woman sitting here to my left?" the attorney asked while gesturing toward Paige. "Get a good look at her, and tell me if you've ever seen her before?"

Acting as if he was scared to look at her, Marcus quickly averted his eyes after glancing at Paige, "Yes, I've seen her before. I used to be friends with one of her daughters."

"And which daughter would that be?" asked the attorney.

"Michelle," said the witness.

Sensing he was on to something, the attorney paused for a moment as he stepped closer, "Let me make sure I got this right, Mr. Myers. You said that you used to be friends with the defendant's daughter, is that correct?"

"Yes."

"Can you please explain to me and the rest of the court why you and Michelle aren't friends anymore?"

"We had an argument a few months ago and she said she didn't want to be friends anymore."

"So, she's the one who ended the friendship?"

"Yes," he said in a low voice.

"Must have been a pretty serious argument?"

"Not to me," he said nonchalantly. "I guess it was to her, though."

"Obviously so if she decided to end the friendship because of it. Do you recall what caused the argument between Michelle and yourself?" the attorney asked as he looked around the courtroom.

"Yes. Her dad and I had a disagreement, and she somehow felt I had disrespected him."

"Why would she think that?" asked the attorney. "I mean, you must have said or done something that she felt was wrong?"

"I didn't do anything," the witness snapped. "He started talking crazy to me for no reason at all, so I said something crazy to him in return."

"Could you share with the court what you said to him?"

"Nothing really. I just told him if he wasn't their dad I would pop a cap in his ass for disrespecting me."

"Mr. Myers, how is that nothing? Isn't popping a cap in someone's ass the same thing as shooting them?"

"Yeah, but I didn't shoot him!" the witness retorted.

"Mr. Myers, is it true that your street name is M-80?" the attorney asked in a calmer voice.

"It's not a street name, it's a nickname," Marcus replied.

"How did you acquire it—who was the first person to call you that?"

"It's just a name that my friends started calling me in elementary school."

"You have a pretty extensive history of violence too, don't you?"

"I guess you could say that. I've had my share of run-ins with the law, but that was a long time ago."

"You're not on trial, so I can only mention that you've had a violent past. I can't mention specifically what your charges were, do you understand?"

"Yes," said Marcus.

While pacing the floor, the attorney cleverly found a way to trap the witness and he desperately wanted his words to resonate with the jurors. "Mr. Myers, it's crazy for a person who has a nickname like M-80, who also has an extensive history of violence to come in here and say that it's only a coincidence that two days after you threatened to shoot Dr. Goldwyn, Dr. Goldwyn just happened to end up dead. Do you really expect this court to believe that?"

"Objection, Your Honor," said the district attorney.

"Overruled," the judge said.

"Do you really think that we're that stupid, Mr. Myers?" Mr. Brown asked.

"Hold up, man!" shouted the witness as he leapt to his feet. "What the hell are you talking about, I've already told you that I didn't shoot that man!"

"*Order, Order!*" the judge screamed while banging his gavel. "That's enough counselor, and you need to be seated, Mr. Myers. I will not tolerate this in my courtroom. One more outburst like that, and I'll be forced to hold you in contempt!"

Marcus Myers was angrily pointing at the defense attorney, still standing on his feet when he yelled at the judge, "He's twisting it up trying to make it look like I killed that man."

"Control yourself young man, and sit down," the judge said before turning to the lawyer who had silenced himself. "Counselor, do you have anything else to ask this witness?"

"Not at this time, Your Honor, but it's clear now why they call him M-80," he said before sitting down.

"The witness is yours, Mr. Burch."

"Thank you, Judge," the prosecutor said as he took the floor. "I only have a few questions for you, Mr. Myers. When you and the deceased had the argument that morning, did you mean it when you said that you would pop a cap in his ass?"

"No. It was said out of anger, but I didn't mean it."

"Mr. Myers, did you ever see Dr. Goldwyn again after that?"

"No."

"You never saw him again?"

"Never."

"That means that you couldn't have killed him, is that correct?"

"That's correct. I had nothing to do with that man's death," the witness said, directing his answer towards Paige's attorney.

"That's all the questions I have, Your Honor," said the district attorney as he went to his seat.

"Will there be a rebuttal?" the judge asked.

"No, Your Honor," Mr. Brown replied.

After removing his glasses, the judge once again turned to the witness-stand, "You're excused, Mr. Myers. When you leave this courtroom do not discuss your testimony with anyone else, do you understand?"

"Yes," he said as he rolled his eyes.

Nearly twenty minutes after Marcus's testimony, Rashad Myers quickly exited the courtroom feeling just as angry as his older brother. While corroborating the story his brother had given, the young man burst into tears on the witness-stand after feeling betrayed by the seasoned attorney.

Knowing he had hurt the prosecution's case, Defense Attorney Donald Brown turned and winked at his client before leaning in closer and whispering to her, "It's your turn to put the nail in the coffin."

Looking every bit of his old age, District Attorney Ricardo Burch looked as if he had been punched in the gut when his opponent stood up and called his next witness.

"Your Honor, I would like to call my client, Paige Goldwyn to the stand."

As if an angel had suddenly appeared from the sky, all eyes in the courtroom quickly shifted in Paige's direction when she rose to her feet and adjusted her skirt. She seemed to feel a sense of empowerment from all the attention as she headed toward the witness-stand, quite confidently, as the bailiff approached her to swear her in.

Meanwhile, her attorney Mr. Brown remained at bay, tactically allowing her presence to linger as he stood beside the table skimming over his notes, "Mrs. Goldwyn, did you love your husband?" he asked without looking at her.

"Of course I did," she answered calmly.

"He provided you with a pretty good life, didn't he?"

"Yes, he did," she said with a smile. "Besides blessing me with our beautiful twin daughters that you saw earlier, we ran a very successful medical practice together and the memories we made will always be priceless."

Her attorney paused, allowing her words to linger before following up with his next question, "Mrs. Goldwyn, what kind of man would you say your husband was? How would you describe him?"

"James was a great man. I couldn't have asked for a better husband, and the girls couldn't have dreamed of having a better father. He was also an intelligent man. Very loving, caring, compassionate and gentle. I can go on and on about how wonderful he was, he was extremely passionate and very attentive."

"In the twenty plus years that you spent with him, did the two of you ever have any physical altercations? Fights, shoving or anything of that nature?" her attorney asked.

"Absolutely not. My husband and I were very loving. We've had countless verbal disagreements, but never anything that came close to physical," she said as tears welled in her eyes.

"Did you kill your husband, Mrs. Goldwyn?" asked the attorney, trying to make a point.

"Absolutely not."

"Mrs. Goldwyn, do you know of anyone who could have possibly wanted to see him dead?"

Taking her time to think about it, Paige closed her eyes and spoke aggressively, "The young man we just saw is the only person who could have killed my husband."

"*Objection*, Your Honor, that's speculative!" the district attorney yelled as he jumped to his feet.

"How is it speculative, Your Honor, when there's testimony that supports the witness' assertion?" Mr. Brown retorted.

"Objection sustained," the judge replied. "The jury is to disregard the last remark made by Mrs. Goldwyn."

"Argumentative, Your Honor," said Mr. Brown.

"Overruled," the judge replied.

Once the colloquy subsided, Mr. Brown strolled over and looked at the jurors before turning around slowly to address his client, "I believe you, Mrs. Goldwyn. I believe you when you say you didn't kill your husband."

Immediately following Mr. Brown's direct-examination, District Attorney Ricardo Burch was up on his feet and in the middle of the courtroom clapping his hands, "Mrs. Goldwyn, that was a very good act you just put on. I mean, it was splendid," he said as he continued clapping. "I have news for you, Mrs. Goldwyn. This jury is a lot smarter than you give them credit for. Do you think that they're going to believe anything that comes out of your mouth?"

"Objection, Your Honor," said Mr. Brown.

"Objection sustained," the judge replied.

"Mrs. Goldwyn, let's be honest here. Did you really love your husband?" the district attorney asked while scratching his head.

"I loved my husband very much."

"Then why'd you kill him?" he asked audaciously.

"I did no such thing," Paige replied as Mr. Brown objected.

"You said a lot of good things about your husband, Mrs. Goldwyn. Did you really mean the things you said about him?"

"I meant everything I said about him. He was a great man."

"Then why'd you kill him!" he repeated.

"Objection, Your Honor, my client has already answered the question."

"Sustained. Watch your step, Mr. Burch. The witness has already answered the question."

"I have no further questions, Your Honor," the district attorney said before sitting down.

"The defense rests, Your Honor," Mr. Brown said from the defense table.

"Thank you, Mrs. Goldwyn. You may go back and sit next to your attorney," the judge instructed while gazing at her. "Well counselor, this definitely went a lot quicker than I expected it to. It's only noon and we've already heard testimony from five witnesses. Quite impressive."

"Thank you, Your Honor," replied the attorney.

"Well, there's no need to delay it. Let's take an hour lunch then come back in and start closing arguments," the judge said as he grabbed his gavel. "Court is adjourned until one PM."

When everyone departed from the courtroom to go eat lunch, Defense Attorney Donald Brown chose to stay behind because he needed a few moments to confer with his client. Her bright smile told him that she was impressed, and he felt so excited when she reached out to hug him.

"Thank you, Mr. Brown—I think we got 'em."

"It's not over yet, sweetie," he replied while embracing her. "It's definitely not over yet."

"I think it's looking good for me, though."

"I think so too, but the outcome of this trial is not up to us. It's up to the jury and whatever they decide."

"Are you ready to do your closing argument?"

"Of course," he said with confidence. "Don't forget he gets to go twice."

"Yeah, I know, but thanks to my silver-tongued attorney, he'll need more than that to win this case," she said, smiling. "I think today's testimony just clenched it for me. You were awesome."

"Thank you," he replied. "I still don't understand why they tried this case. They have no murder weapon, no witnesses or anything. Hopefully we did enough to win over the jury because it would really break my heart if we lose this thing."

"Why?"

"Because your daughters are counting on me, and nothing will make me happier than to see you go home to them, especially after the massage they gave me over the weekend. I feel it's the least I can do for them," he said gratuitously.

Playfully nudging his arm, Paige burst out laughing as she replied, "Yeah, they told me about that. I don't think I'll be found guilty though. I didn't do anything, so I really don't see that happening to me."

"I know, and I don't think you'll be found guilty either. That's one of the advantages of having a speedy trial. It doesn't give them enough time to build a rock-solid case against you. That's one of the reasons they don't have a case," he said as he closed his briefcase. "A lot of people make the mistake of waiving their right to a speedy trial. Then, when they're found guilty, they sit there wondering what happened, and their lawyer sits there pretending like he's just as surprised."

"I'm glad you have my best interest at heart."

"I do. Not only that, but instead of me having my investigators do all of the legwork for me, I went out and did the majority of it myself. Let's not get too ahead of ourselves, though, because we still don't know what's going to happen," he said as he stood up. "Go eat lunch, and I'll see you again in a lil' while."

Before leaving the courtroom, he waved his hand to get the guard's attention—his client was escorted to a holding-cell where her lunch was waiting.

Straightening the lapels on his expensive suit-jacket, Defense Attorney Donald Brown had a look of anguish spread across his face as he looked at the prosecutor out the corner of his eyes. The prosecutor had just concluded his first summation and it was clear to everyone, including the judge, that the defense attorney had been deeply affected by it. He had one hand placed inside of his pants pocket as he peered down at the floor, carefully placing one foot in front of the other as he inched his way toward the jury box. The jurors stared at him, seemingly studying his face, it was obvious they wanted to know what the man was thinking. Without saying a word, the defense attorney demanded their undivided attention—his dominant presence displayed nothing but confidence.

"Ladies and gentlemen of the jury," he said as he scanned their faces, wanting to be certain he had their attention. "The DA just gave you this spiel about how guilty my client is and why you should find her guilty for the charge of murder. Let me explain why she is not guilty and why you should ignore the prosecutor's assertion and come back with a verdict of not guilty."

He noticed the prosecutor sit up in his chair then cross his arms, possibly attempting to convey a message to the jury through body language, "Mr. Burch has not presented one shred of evidence in this case. No murder weapon, no eyewitnesses, no motive—no nothing. He has proven absolutely nothing, but in his closing argument, he talks about how my client only wanted her husband's money and how she probably used her beauty and charm to win his heart, deceptively hiding her real motive for marrying him. That's absurd. Let's not forget that they were high school sweethearts. He didn't have any money when they fell in love. The prosecutor must have forgotten that fact?" he said as he leaned against the plaintiff's table. "Ladies and gentlemen, this is a court of law. A place where facts and evidence speaks louder than words—a place where justice is supposed to prevail. This is not a place to play guessing games or make off-the-wall insinuations, especially if you don't have the evidence to back it up," he said candidly. "Mr. Burch made a few indirect comments, suggesting my client thought that she could get away with murder because she's a beautiful white woman and no one would care or believe that she could be responsible for killing a black man. To me, that suggests racism. Mr. Burch is playing a game of manipulation. He's trying to plant in your minds that this is a case about race. He's doing it because it's common practice in every courtroom across the country and he's had a lot of success with it in the past—even in cases like these where he lack evidence. Let's be honest, if my client was a black woman accused of killing a rich white man—she would have already been adjudicated guilty in your minds, long before she stepped foot inside of this courtroom. We see it everyday in this country. That's because racism is the American way. That's the way things are done in the United States and that's the way it has always been. That's why, with no evidence at all to support his allegations, Mr. Burch feels comfortable relying on racism alone to win a conviction in a case as weak as this. He has done it countless times when the victim was white and the defendant was black, and he is counting on it to work for him again."

"*Objection*, Your Honor!" the district attorney yelled. "Mr. Brown is deliberately trying to mislead the jury. The assertions he's making are clearly inaccurate."

"Overruled," the judge replied.

Before continuing his argument, Attorney Donald Brown walked over to the defense table and took a sip of water—delighted to see that he'd gotten under the prosecutor's skin. He knew he had Mr. Burch exactly where he wanted him, and he had no intentions of letting up.

He strolled to the center of the courtroom, impelling everyone's eyes to follow closely—hoping his words would possess the impact he desired when he stopped in his tracks and began speaking, "Intelligent men and women of the jury. Let me explain something to you as briefly as possible about this beautiful country we call America. There is no secret that racism is bred in this country. It always has been and it probably always will, but that doesn't mean that it has to be. It's like that because we choose to follow other people's minds instead of our own. We have rights in this country, and with those rights comes the ability to make our own decisions. We don't have to follow the trends and ideologies others have followed before us. We all know that racism is wrong. It has always been wrong and I think everyone in America is finally starting to realize it," he said while looking at the jurors. "Look at me," he said while poking his chest with his finger. "I'm proof that this country believes in change. I grew up in Mississippi in the Jim Crow days, and as hard as it was for black folks, my parents still believed that it was possible to put me through college and law school. Even with all the roadblocks and obstacles that were in place, preventing black people from achieving success—they still believed in this country we call America. The same way that my parents believed, that's the same belief I have in all of you, and I trust you'll do the right thing and ignore the color of my client and the victim in this case, and base your judgment on the evidence presented—or the lack thereof. As Americans we have the responsibility to do what's right, regardless of how people with the good ol'boy mentality may feel about it. Color should never play a role in a court of law, or anywhere else for that matter. I think the majority of people in this country agrees, that's why Barack Obama was elected the first black president of the United States. That's proof that color can be ignored because it was ignored in that case. And, in this case, since the DA has failed to prove that my client is guilty of any wrongdoing, you must find her not guilty for the charge of murder. Listen, my fellow Americans, this is your moment—this is your time. It's your chance to prove that fair trials can be received in the United States. You twelve jurors are the real symbols of this country. It's not Lady Justice. Lady Justice is a false symbol of this country. She tricks Americans into believing that justice is blind. The blindfold is a throw off—and the scale of justice is so unbalanced it's unbelievable. But, black people know better. We know that we're not treated equally by white people or the justice system in America—and regardless of how bad it sounds, I'm only saying it because it's true. We experience racism every day in this country, and we're forced to keep finding ways to get through it. Let's prove that we have what it takes to do the right thing. Let's prove it by finding my client not guilty for the charge of murder."

Silence hovered over the courtroom when the attorney took a seat. Everyone was speechless. They had all been touched in one way or another by the closing argument, and since Prosecutor Ricardo Burch had put the race-card on the table, the defense attorney chose to keep it there—using reverse psychology. Jurors were sneaking peeks at each other during the closing argument, now they all found themselves anxious to see how the prosecutor was going to respond. Even the judge showed interest when the man finally stood up and took the floor.

"Don't be fooled by Mr. Brown's argument, ladies and gentlemen," he said as he avoided making eye contact. "This is an open and shut case. Color has nothing at all to do with this trial. Mr. Brown's argument was more like a Dr. King speech. It has no business being made in a murder trial," he said while pacing the floor. "I would see the relevance in it if he was running for some kind of political office or something, but I think that the speech was very inappropriate for a court of law. Paige Goldwyn is guilty of murder. The evidence I presented is proof of that!" he said while pointing his finger in her direction. "Doctor James Goldwyn has already suffered enough. Please let's not make him a victim twice. It's true that this case was largely built on circumstantial evidence, but whether it's circumstantial or not, it is still evidence and it is perfectly legal in a court of law. No, we don't have the murder weapon, we don't have any eyewitnesses to the crime, but Doctor James Goldwyn should not suffer because of it. His wife was the only person in bed with him the night he died. She's the only one who knows exactly what happened. She's the only witness to the crime. That's because she's responsible for killing him—now it's up to you to make her pay. I also believe in our great country, America, and I also believe in all of you. Great men and women of the jury, Mrs. Goldwyn is guilty. I'm sure of it—just as I'm sure we're all sitting in this courtroom, so please come back with a verdict of guilty."

After the attorneys completed their closing arguments, Judge Yen Miyasato gave jury instructions, "It's still quite early ladies and gentlemen. You can convene tonight for a couple of hours, and reconvene in the morning if you don't reach a verdict," he said before adjourning the court.

As deliberations were about to begin, Paige felt her heart sink to the bottom of her chest—her fate now lie in the hands of the jury.

As they all filed out of the courtroom led by the bailiff, not a single juror looked in Paige's direction, causing her to be even more concerned. The jurors entered the small deliberating room and gathered around the table in no specific order. Shortly thereafter, because of the strength she'd shown throughout the trial, they chose forty-five-year-old, Erma Dotson, a black supervisor at a well-known communications company to be the jury's foreperson.

CHAPTER 18

"What the …?" Amp said when he turned around and caught his daughter staring at him.

"Dad, what are you doing?" asked Jada.

"That's the question that I should be asking you. You know no one is allowed to enter my bedroom without knocking first."

"Why are you crying, and what's that for?" she said, pointing to the stacks of money she'd seen him counting.

Amp grabbed his daughter and held her tightly, hoping to stop his little princess from asking more questions, "I love you, ma-ma. I don't know what I would do if I ever lost you."

"I love you too, daddy," she said with a whimper. "I'm sorry for coming in without knocking, but Chyna sent me up here to check on you."

"Tell her that I'll be down there in a couple of minutes," he said as he released his grip.

It hadn't been long since they had come back from Bull's funeral and Amp still didn't know how he was going to make it. He wasn't even sure if he wanted to continue with life, that's the thought he was pondering when Jada entered his bedroom. He turned and looked at the large amount of cash he had spread across his bed. He didn't like the fact that Jada had seen it, but at least she hadn't seen him when he was sitting there holding the loaded 40 caliber pistol against his temple, seriously contemplating on whether he should pull the trigger. He stacked the large denominational bills neatly inside the safe that sat beside his bed then went down to the living room to join his company.

"Anthony, are you okay?" Chyna asked with Jada sitting beside her.

"Yeah, I'm cool. It's a struggle but I'll be alright."

He walked over to the large kitchen area and greeted Missy, Amanda and Veronica as they sat at the table drinking soda.

"Amp, who is that guy that I keep seeing you with?" said Missy.

"Who?"

"The white guy who's always wearing the dark shades. You talked to him at the funeral today and I've seen him at Topnotch a few times. He always looks angry every time I see him."

"Oh, him. That ain't nobody."

"He looks like a cop," said Missy.

"He is, but he don't mean no harm," Amp lied before hurrying away.

The man Missy was referring to was a retired detective. He claimed that he was only following someone else's orders but he had been popping up regularly in different locations trying to extort Amp out of bundles of money. The man was a crook and had threatened to harm Amp and his daughter if he ever went to the police to report anything. Now that Missy had brought it up, Amp had really grown tired of the increasing pressure, and he knew it was time to do what was necessary to protect his daughter.

As she applied strawberry lip gloss to her soft succulent lips, Alix Onefeather felt slightly embarrassed when she noticed that her client was staring at her. With Paige being on trial for her husband's murder, not only had the twins been attending the trial, but she'd closed down the parlor to attend it herself. Now she found herself in an awkward position because she didn't have rent which was due in a week.

Uncertain about how to explain the situation to Mark, Alix caught herself blushing as she stood in the mirror as the old man continued to gaze at her. The two had been friends for several years. So, as he lay on his back with his towel wrapped around him, she realized the look she saw in his eyes was definitely one she had never seen before. Unbeknownst to her, but for the first time in a long time, his entire body was overcome with desire and it caused an erection he didn't know he could have. Impotence had taken away something very important to him. He had almost forgot what it felt like to feel like a man, so as he lay on his back not knowing what to say, he opened his towel and wrapped his hand around his erection and began rubbing the stiffness, feeling truly uplifted. Who would have thought that the sight of Alix's ass and watching her pretty-up her lips would be the perfect antidote for his years of impotence?

"Oh my god," she said when she turned toward him.

"I'm thinking the same thing," he replied frantically. "It's been so long since I've had one of these—I would hate to see it go to waste without putting it to use."

Stepping towards him with long sexy strides, Alix Onefeather never averted her eyes as she stared at his manhood as it stood at attention.

"Mark, I'm baffled. I've never looked at you this way before," she said as she stood beside him and stroked it gently. "There's something that I really need to talk to you about."

"What is it, darling?" said Mark.

"I don't have the money to pay the rent on the parlor this month," she said tentatively. "You know the twins have been attending their moms' trial, and my clientele alone can't cover the rent."

"Don't worry about it. I'll take care of it," he said before gasping.

"Mark, you've already done so much for me, I can't let you keep spending your money on me."

"Alix, would you please shut up so I can concentrate?" he demanded. "If it'll make you feel better to earn the money, then focus your attention on making me come."

With no hesitation, Alix removed her hand from his swollen genitals and skillfully replaced it with her talented mouth. Soon after taking it down her throat, Mark's entire body began to stiffen as he grunted loudly and reached climax.

"Yuck. That's disgusting!" she said as she spit into the towel that lay beside him. "I cannot believe I just did that."

"I have no complaints my little Indian beauty," he replied jokingly. "For the short time it lasted, you were great."

"I still can't believe I just did that," she repeated. "After telling me repeatedly about your impotency, I just thought I'd help you enjoy your erection since it's been so long since you've had one. What if I healed you?" she said, laughing.

"That would be great," he replied with optimism. "I guess looking at you finally got the best of me. You have the sexiest lips and the nicest little bottom I've ever seen. I should have paid attention to it long before now."

"Stop before you embarrass me," she said shyly.

"There's no need to be embarrassed, sweetheart."

"Mark, I'm just kidding. With all of the things you've done for me, it feels good to finally be able to do something for you."

He playfully smacked her on the ass before replying, "That's my girl."

"Watch yourself, old man. I don't want to be responsible if you hurt yourself," she joked.

Out of nowhere, Mark suddenly decided to change the subject, "What's the latest you've heard about the Goldwyn case. Do you think it's possible that she killed her husband?"

"Hell no!" she said emphatically. "Mrs. Goldwyn could have never done anything like that. You should have seen how they acted around each other. I have never seen two people so in love," she said passionately. "Meagan talked to Michelle last night, and according to her, the jury has already begun deliberating."

"Already?" said Mark.

"I know, that's what I said, but they said things are really looking good for her."

"I haven't watched the news today so I don't know. I hope it turns out good for her. I would hate to see those girls lose both of their parents."

Wholeheartedly agreeing, Alix stood in ponder before she spoke, "I know. I think it'll all be fine, though. At least that's what I'm hoping."

"Well, I think I better be getting out of here," said Mark. "I've been here long enough and we don't need Meagan getting suspicious of us."

"Just to be safe, you should bring her a new camera the next time you come. You know how she loves taking pictures."

"Will we do that again the next time I come?" he asked, laughing. "I'm just joking, Alix, so please don't be mad at me. I really enjoyed spending time with you, and I thank you for making me feel young again."

"Get out of here, Mark," she said while shoving him gently. "You better not go running your mouth either, and I'll stop by later to pick up that money."

"Come pick it up whenever you want," he said as he got dressed.

Immediately after Mark made his exit, Alix grabbed her mouthwash from a nearby drawer and ran straight to the bathroom to rinse out her mouth. Although the problem with rent had been resolved, she found it somewhat hard to face herself in the mirror—knowing that what had just happened between her and Mark, she would never allow to happen again.

CHAPTER 19

"Dubai?" said Chyna.

"Yep," Amp replied. "I've already re-searched it and I think it's the best place for us to relocate. The arrangements have already been made."

"Why not Miami or Hawaii or somewhere like that?" Veronica chimed in.

"Girl, those places are played out," said Amanda. "I think Dubai would be good for all of us. There's nothing better than a fresh place when you're looking for a fresh start."

"And, look. It says that they have the tallest building in the world. It's a thousand feet taller than the Empire State Building," Chyna said, still flipping through the pages of the brochure.

"Well, ladies. I guess it's time to make it happen. Stack as much money as you can within the next week, until it's time for us to get out of here," Amp said as he sat in his office, reclined in his chair. He felt like he was on top of the world—truly impressed with his employee's loyalty. He announced that TopNotch Entertainment would be going out of business, for reasons he didn't care to discuss with them. To his surprise, all six girls agreed to go with him so they could set up shop in a new location. He was extremely pleased with the six girls—but was more pleased with Bull, because he had been the one who'd hired them.

CHAPTER 20

On the third floor of the Clark County Detention Center, Wednesdays were usually the most dreaded day for the majority of the women in the D-module. It was the only day of the week that nothing was happening. No personal visits, no commissary, and nothing really on television that was worth tuning in to. The only alternatives were to mope around the module, talk on the phone, or play cards or board games to pass the time. However, this Wednesday was different. Paige Goldwyn had been called back to District Court because the jury in her murder trial had reached a verdict. Most of the women who had been there a while had taken a liking to Paige and they were really anxious to hear what the results were. Her two closest friends, Tangie and Chrissy were sitting in the rear of the module bowing their heads in prayer while the rest of the women gathered around the television set. They all believed in their friend's innocence, and they hoped that the jury would feel the same.

As they waited impatiently inside the module, Paige Goldwyn sat jittery inside the cold courtroom, wondering how her attorney could sit so emotionless, "You must have balls of steel? Here I am shaking like a leaf and you're sitting there calm like nothing is happening."

Without looking at his client, Mr. Brown stayed composed, displaying control at its highest level, "I don't think there's anything to be worried about."

"I guess that's easy for you to say since you know that you're going home regardless, huh? I don't know if I'm going home or to prison for the rest of my life," she said as if it was all his fault.

"You make it sound so much worse than it really is. The district attorney has failed miserably to prove his case, and if by chance you are found guilty, I can almost guarantee you we'll win on appeal," he said as he fixed his tie. "There is absolutely no evidence to support a guilty verdict."

"Let's hope the jury sees it that way," said Paige.

"They have no choice if they followed the instructions that the judge gave them. Murder is one of the hardest charges to prove, and the only thing that they've proven is that they have no case," he said before she cut him off.

"Oh shit, here they come," she said nervously. "Please, God, don't let them send me to prison."

As if de'ja' vu was taking place, each juror filed into the jury box with their head hanging low, giving no indication as to what they'd decided. Just as she'd done when they left the courtroom to deliberate, Paige stared at each of the twelve jurors as they took their seat, hoping to get some kind of clue as to how they had voted.

"Has the jury reached a verdict?" the judge asked after they sat down.

"Yes we have, Your Honor," the forewoman replied.

After reviewing the verdict form he received from the bailiff, Judge Miyasato swiftly handed it back then cleared his throat and faced the defendant, "Please rise, Mrs. Goldwyn and stand next to your attorney," he said before pausing. "Go ahead and read the verdict, please."

As Erma Dotson slowly unfolded the paper, everyone in the courtroom were on pins and needles as she stared at the verdict with a blank expression, "For the charge of first-degree murder, we the jury finds the defendant, Paige Goldwyn—not guilty."

It was pandemonium at that moment—every woman in the D-module yelled with excitement. Meanwhile, Paige sat breathless inside of the courtroom as she leaned her head against her attorney's shoulder. The instant she heard the verdict, her entire body felt so relieved, as if the entire world had been lifted from her shoulders, "Thank you, Mr. Brown. Thank you so much," she said as she burst into tears.

"I told you that there was nothing to worry about," he replied as he held her closely.

When Michelle and Melissa rushed to hug their mother, the prosecutor acknowledged them through beady-red eyes as he pushed his way through the crowd to leave the courtroom.

Detective Bruno, who had taken a seat on the back row, stood up displaying a broad smile when he saw the deep sadness on the prosecutor's face. He slipped on his shades and pulled down his hat before blending in quietly with the rest of the crowd.

UNFAIR

Paige hoped to leave the courtroom with her beautiful daughters, instead, she had to return to the jail and await the courts order to process her out.

The verdict had only been read two hours prior when the two attorneys met up at a tavern on the outskirts of town.

"Hey, Ricardo."

"Hi, Donald. I received your text message saying to meet you here. What's up?" the DA said as he climbed on the barstool.

"I don't know. I was kind of hoping you could tell me."

"Are you talking about this latest case?"

"That's exactly what I'm talking about. Is it me, or did this case seem strange to you?"

"Well, Donald, since you brought it up, this case was different from the very beginning."

"How so?"

"I'm more than sure you already know since you're the one who brought it up."

"Ricardo, I'm a defense lawyer and I get paid decent money to provide a service. However, my oath to practice law in an ethical manner means more to me than anything. I know how bad your office wants to tear my head off and eat it because none of you guys have been able to beat me in trial. But, Ricardo, I've faced you many times in several different courtrooms and you have never tried a case as weak as this. My question to you is; why did you

157

try this case and why was your performance so mediocre?"

"Donald, this case was bigger than us. A lot bigger. I received orders from up top—telling me that I had to try this case and not plea it out. These orders came from some very prominent people so I didn't bother questioning it once it was put to me. Also, my office was ransacked before the trial began, plus my computer was hacked into and it seems that they were only interested in the Goldwyn files."

"Did you report it?"

"Hell no, I didn't report it. I couldn't report it. No one could have broken into my office or hacked into my computer unless they had some connections in some very high places."

"I didn't know all of that was taking place but I knew that something peculiar was going on with this case. What are your plans now?" asked the defense attorney.

"I plan to leave this case alone and I strongly suggest that you do the same thing. It wouldn't be wise to challenge the powers that be and we wouldn't be safe if we did so."

"There's no recourse?"

"None whatsoever. This case is over."

"Will you keep practicing law after this?" asked the attorney.

"Do you think that I would quit before whipping your ass? Never. It will always be my goal to beat you in court and I wouldn't dare quit the DA's office before I accomplish that. Are you crazy?"

"You're a good man, Ricardo," Mr. Brown smiled. "Obviously you're a smart man, too because you know how to let bygones be bygones. This is our career—our livelihood, and if someone took these kind of measures to dictate a case, I think the best thing for us to do is to let it be."

"Smart man, Donald," the DA said while patting his shoulder. "That's the decision I was hoping you'd make, and I promise to whip your ass the next time we face each other in court."

"Keep dreaming, Ricardo. Keep dreaming."

The attorneys shook hands then parted ways. Their decision to leave the Goldwyn case alone was not based on right and wrong, it was more so based on life or death.

CHAPTER 21

O n the top floor of the Bellagio Hotel, several maids heard screams coming from the Penthouse Suite as they stood in the hallway waiting to enter the elevator. Paige had been brought here immediately by Detective Bruno when she was released from jail a few hours before. They hadn't wasted much time getting down to business because the detective was not one to procrastinate.

With the hand-crafted drapes pulled all the way open, a glimmer of daybreak was becoming more visible as Paige lay on her back with her legs in the air as the detective performed cunnilingus on her, "Oh yes, baby. That's it!" she screamed while clutching the bed. Her lower body began to tremble as she reached orgasm for the second time.

She lay in bed smiling from ear to ear, overflowing with joy after being acquitted of her husband's murder. No words could describe her exuberance. She felt totally rejuvenated after being incarcerated for nearly four months.

Detective Bruno was sweating profusely when he crawled from

between her legs and laid beside her. She wiped the sweat from his forehead and kissed him softly before lying his head against her ample breasts. She had often fantasized about him while sitting in jail and wondered what it would be like to make love to him. Quite often she'd found herself thinking about it late at night when she longed to be held by a masculine man.

From the moment they arrived at the elegant hotel, there was nothing but laughter and total bliss as they pleasured each other in more ways than one, "You turned out to be even better than I thought you'd be," she said while stroking his hair.

"Likewise."

"I think it's time that I get home to my girls," said Paige.

"Let's have breakfast first and I would be more than happy to take you home."

"Room service," she asked.

"Sounds great to me," he said before kissing her cheek.

An hour later, once they'd eaten and took a shower, Paige Goldwyn and Detective Bruno were on the expressway headed for Southern Highlands. After reaching her home, she thanked him respectively for all he'd done before exiting the vehicle and seeing him off. Although they hadn't made plans to see each other again, she knew in her heart that it wouldn't be the last she would see of him. She stood there for a moment in the middle of the street—enjoying the sunlight, appreciating the beauty of being free again when a teardrop fell from her sparkling blue eyes—sensing her late husband's spirit surrounding her. Dr. James Goldwyn had meant the world to her. And, after all the years they spent together, she now found herself feeling guilty because she had spread her legs for another man—something she knew he wouldn't approve of.

It was just after seven AM when she entered the house, and to her surprise, her daughters were already up waiting for her.

"Mom!" Michelle screamed. "Where have you been, we have been up for hours waiting for you?" she cried as they embraced each other. "I called the jail and they said that you were released at two o'clock this morning."

Knowing she couldn't tell them the truth, Paige felt she had no choice but to lie to her daughters, "A friend of mine took me to breakfast."

"It's so good to have you back home. We miss you," Melissa said with tears in her eyes.

"I miss you guys, too. Very much."

The three women went into the kitchen where coffee was brewing and spent the next hour and a half getting reacquainted. They had talked on the phone nearly every day while Paige was in jail but it seemed they still had a lot of catching up to do. They discussed everything that happened while she was away, especially the things in the neighborhood. Michelle talked about Bull's death like she was happy about it, but suddenly switched the subject when she looked at the clock, "We really hate to leave you mom, but we have to get ready to go to work. If you'd like, you could always come down to get a free massage. I'm sure you could probably use one, right?"

A massage would be great, Paige told herself. But for reasons only she understood, she knew that she had to decline her daughter's offer, "I'm fine, sweetie. Thanks anyway. I would rather stay home and relax awhile."

"Will you be okay being here by yourself?" asked Melissa.

"Sure, honey. I just need to get used to being home again. I am so glad to be out of that place. It's no place for anyone to be, although I did meet a lot of nice women while I was there."

When Michelle and Melissa ran upstairs, they never even noticed that their mom had stayed at the bottom of the staircase trying to suppress her emotions after being bombarded with depressing memories. Paige took a deep breath and exhaled it slowly then ascended the stairs one step at a time until she reached the bedroom she'd shared with her husband. This was the last place she'd seen him alive, and after stepping inside and closing the door, the pain she felt deep inside her heart could no longer be contained as she fell to her knees and began sobbing.

Later that evening, the lobby of the A-One massage parlor was finally at peace after a long busy day of total chaos. The business had been flooded with new walk-in clients and a large group of local reporters whose only interest was to get a story.

"I can't believe how crazy it's been," Alix said while looking at the twins. "In one day, I think you girls made up for all the days you've missed. I'm glad that your mom is finally out because it's good to see you both happy again."

"I know. It seems like when they're happy everybody's happy," said Meagan.

"If all these reporters were here just to see the two of you, imagine how it would be if your mom was here? My parlor would become famous after that."

"My mom's not coming," Michelle replied. "I told her she could come down to get a free massage, but she said that she would rather stay at home."

"She said that?" asked Alix.

"Yeah, do you blame her? Wouldn't you wanna stay at home if you just finished going through all of that?"

"Yeah, I guess," said Alix, knowing that Michelle was probably right. "But, now that she's been acquitted, that still leaves your father's murder unsolved."

A stone-coldness was seen in Michelle's eyes when she clenched her teeth and began speaking, "We know who did it. Marcus is the only bastard who could have killed our father."

"I don't know if he did it or not, but we need to find out who killed our dad," Melissa said. "I don't even want to think about it right now, the important thing is that our mom is home."

"That's true," said Meagan. "Now let's count this money."

Once the money was counted and divided equally, the four women were all exhausted but they left the parlor with a look of contentment. While Meagan and Alix chose to go out for drinks, Michelle and Melissa rode home in silence, both asking themselves who killed their dad.

CHAPTER 22

Early Friday morning, Andrea Shaw was in deep thought as she sat near the nightstand smoking a blunt. Wearing her sexy black g-string with a strapless bra, she was on the verge of waking up Marcus because his loud snoring had really started to irritate her. Still upset about an argument they had the night before, she was tempted to pack her things and leave the apartment since she wasn't certain they would have a future together. She was of the opinion that she and Marcus should go ahead and get married so that her daughters could be raised in a conventional family. Marcus, however, had a different opinion. Although he loved her daughters, he had been quick to express his misogamist views, which was shocking to her, because she had no idea that he didn't believe in marriage. He responded by saying marriage did not run in his family and it wasn't in his blood to settle down with one woman for the rest of his life.

As she sat on the bed with one leg beneath her, Andrea felt herself getting upset all over again so she put the blunt to her lips and deeply inhaled. She held the smoke in her lungs for as long as she could, and began coughing as she slowly exhaled, and was gasping for air when the phone rang, "Hello," she said while panting.

"Who is this?" the caller asked.

"Who did you call to speak to?" asked Andrea.

"Is Rashad there?"

"He is, but he's still asleep. Would you like for me to go wake him up?"

"Yes, please," said the caller.

"And who should I say is calling?"

"Tell him it's Melissa."

Lying the phone on the nightstand next to her jewelry, Andrea slowly got up from the bed and put the blunt to her lips before heading up the stairs to Rashad's bedroom. Without knocking, she pushed the door open and woke him up and was surprised to see how anxious he became when she told him Melissa was on the phone waiting to talk to him. She watched as he made a half-hearted attempt to conceal his excitement, but she could tell that he really wanted to talk to Melissa. Andrea knew that Rashad wasn't rude and arrogant like his older brother. So, instead of leaving his bedroom, she faked like she was going to leave by walking toward the door, hoping she could make him feel like he was being put under hypnosis as her ass cheeks jiggled from side to side. She knew that Marcus would have a fit if he found out she was parading around the apartment in her underwear, but she wasn't the least bit concerned about how he'd feel. To her, her shapely ass was one of her best features and she could tell that Rashad was really turned on by it. She knew his heart was probably set on talking to Melissa but his eyes were on her when she turned around. She smiled at Rashad and waived at him before leaving his bedroom so he could talk in private.

"Hello," he said in a deep voice.

As soon as Melissa heard his voice, she immediately began asking questions, "Who is that bitch you got answering the phone?"

"Damn! What happened to hello or how you doin'? You haven't talked to me in weeks and the first thing you ask is who is that bitch?"

"Hi, Rashad. How are you, now who is that girl that answered the phone?"

"Girl, your ass is crazy," he said smiling. "That was Andrea, my brother's girlfriend. I heard the good news about your mom."

"Yeah, she's finally out," said Melissa.

"That's good, I know you're happy as hell, huh?"

"You know I am."

"So, what made you decide to call me after all this time?"

"I was wondering if we could get together sometime this weekend? We need to talk," Melissa replied.

"About what," asked Rashad.

"You'll find out when the time comes."

"You're not pregnant, are you?"

"No, it's nothing like that. Do you think we'll be able to get together or what?"

"You know you got that. I made plans to do something with my brother tonight, so it'll probably have to be tomorrow or Sunday."

"That's fine. I'll check back with you tomorrow or Sunday then."

"Alright," he said, realizing at that moment how much he missed her.

"It's good hearing your voice, Rashad, and I guess I'll be talking to you again soon."

"It's good hearing your voice, too. And, thanks for calling," he said before hanging up.

The call went a lot smoother than she thought it would. Melissa knew that she still had feelings for Rashad, but getting justice for her dad was much more important, so she had to find a way to push her feelings aside. Once the call was complete, she stood with one hand on her hip, knowing she had to figure out how to get some answers.

Paige weaved her white Mercedes Benz in and out of traffic and almost side-swiped a truck as it pulled up beside her. The afternoon sun was heating up, and since Decatur Boulevard was a known high-traffic area, she really wanted to reach her destination as quickly as possible. Detective Bruno had called her earlier that morning and they agreed to meet at Red Lobster for lunch while he was on break.

As soon as she pulled into the parking lot and parked beside him, she noticed that he was leaning against his truck waiting for her, but was quickly at her side assisting her as she pushed the door open to get out of her car, "You're late, but you're stunning," he said as he grabbed her hand.

"Thank you. I sort of got stuck in traffic," she replied, noticing he hadn't taken his eyes off her.

"That's okay, we still have plenty of time," he said as they walked toward the entrance.

He got behind her and couldn't keep himself from staring as her skirt clung tightly to her pear-shaped hips. To him, Paige Goldwyn was perfect in every way and he knew that he could never get enough of her.

After going inside and being seated, they enjoyed a small appetizer of shrimp cocktail before deciding on sharing a seafood salad. They wanted something that wouldn't take long to prepare and would be easy to consume since the detective only had an hour for lunch.

As they stared at each other from across the table, he recognized the look she had in her eyes to be the same one she'd given him the day they met, "How does it feel to be free again?" he asked while kissing her hand.

"It's great, but I have so much catching up to do. After you called this morning, the girls had already left for work, so I got up and called myself cleaning the house but ended up setting a lot of things aside that I've decided to donate to the Salvation Army," she continued. "Mostly James' things, but I'll need to get rid of it eventually."

"Sounds like you've been pretty busy?" he said, acting as though he was really interested. "You should be relaxing for a week or two."

"I wish," she smiled. "And, that's just the beginning of it. After I took a shower and had breakfast, I took my car and had it washed because it accumulated so much dust just sitting in the garage. Then I went to pay some bills since the computer is broken and ended up getting a few money orders for some friends I met in jail. You have no idea how tired I am."

"You'll be okay," he assured her.

"Oh, I know. I just need to get used to running around again. I feel all yucky after being in there," she said while looking around, trying to make sure no one was eavesdropping. "I need a full-body massage and the whole nine yards. If you can think of it I probably need it."

"All I need is you, sweetheart," he said smoothly.

"Thank you," she blushed.

"Why not go to A-One and get a massage?" he asked while caressing her hands.

"Oh no, I can't go there," she answered quickly. "My daughters suggested it yesterday but I would be very uncomfortable going down there. I thought you said you would take me to Tahiti Village?"

"Oh god, that place is beautiful," he said with a glare in his eyes. "We'll for surely have to make that happen when I go on vacation in a couple of weeks."

"I hope it's as lovely as you say it is."

"Oh, believe me it is. It's strictly for couples and I know you're gonna love it once we get out there."

"I can't wait to go," she said.

"And, I can't wait to take you."

Just before the waitress sat their food on the table, Detective Bruno's demeanor became a lot more serious as he asked her some questions he'd been dying to know, "Paige, have you told your daughters about us yet, and do you see us having a future together?"

She picked up her fork and began eating, purposely ignoring the questions he posed to her. He had never been made to feel so small and was truly offended when he pulled back the seafood salad and repeated the same two questions he had just asked.

Seeing he was persistent, she slammed her fork on the table and stared at him, "Frank, I can't tell my daughters about us. Hearing something like that would destroy them," she said while shaking. "Besides, I wouldn't feel comfortable with them being around you. I wouldn't mind if you and I continue seeing each other, but I really can't see us having a future together."

"What!" he said, trying to control his voice. "What are you talking about? You know you really have a lot of nerve, Paige! You want us to continue sleeping together but you don't want us to have a relationship?" he said with his jowls trembling. "And, what do you mean you would be uncomfortable having your daughters around me?"

"Frank, you're a racist!" she stated bluntly. "You don't like black people, remember? They wouldn't be anything but niggers to you, or have you forgotten that my daughters are black?"

"C'mon, Paige, you know that's not fair. I have never said anything derogatory about your daughters, and I would never do anything to hurt them."

"What's the difference? You've said derogatory things about their dad, and I bet you wouldn't have hesitated to hurt him, would you? For no other reason than him being black," she said before pausing. "Frank, it shouldn't be difficult for you to understand. I love my daughters, and as a mother, I can't have you around my babies when I know how you feel about black people. What kind of mother would I be if I did that?"

"I don't believe this," he said while lowering his head. "You really blew me away with this. I mistakenly thought we liked each other. Well, I guess I'll go ahead and leave. Would you mind if I call you later?"

"Do whatever you like," she whispered.

Detective Bruno returned to his car in the parking lot, face flushed with anger as he reflected on the words they'd just exchanged. When he crawled inside his car and glanced at the Mercedes parked next to him, the thought crossed his mind to set it on fire but he burst out laughing for conjuring up the thought. He knew that he had fallen in love with Paige. She was everything he'd ever wanted in a woman and he was hoping she would feel the same way about him. He started the engine, threw his car in reverse— wishing he had never crossed the boundaries of sleeping with her.

It was eight-thirty PM and Paige planned to be in bed no later than nine. She was becoming more and more upset with Amp because he hadn't picked up his daughter like he had promised, nor had he bothered to call to provide an explanation. Paige felt he was taking her kindness for weakness, because he was over an hour late, and she still hadn't heard a word from him.

Being a mother of two herself, her heart couldn't help but go out to Amp after he explained what happened to Jada's mom Nikki in Seattle, Washington, and why his eight-year-old daughter had to come live with him. Prior to moving to Vegas, Jada had been forced to live with her ailing grandmother in the State of Washington, who simply could no longer afford to care for her. Her mother Nikki was currently in a Burn Center in Seattle suffering from third-degree burns that covered more than eighty-percent of her body after being dowsed with gasoline and set on fire by a jealous boyfriend who suspected her of cheating.

Paige was heart-broken after hearing the story and she offered to help in any way she could. She was already feeling empathy for him because they had just finished discussing what happened to Bull and how ironic it was for them to both lose loved ones to violence in such close proximity. At that time, he said that he had to go handle some important business, so out of the kindness of her heart, she volunteered to baby-sit Jada if he needed her to. That was at three o'clock PM.

Now she found herself in a dilemma—she wondered if he was taking advantage of her. She hoped that he was okay because those actions were abnormal for the Anthony she'd come to know. It was uncharacteristic of him to take her for granted so she really didn't know what to think of it. It was now nine-twenty and there was still no word from Jada's father. His whereabouts seemed to be the farthest thing from Jada's mind as she lay across the floor playing Nintendo.

Paige continued to watch the clock. The thought entered her mind to call his cell phone again but she had already called twice and he didn't answer. She decided to just go over there, even though she knew that he wasn't home. She helped Jada gather up all of her belongings and, together, they marched next door where they saw a large moving van parked in front of the house. She couldn't believe it as she watched Amp and two other men use dollys to load large cardboard boxes inside the truck. She had no idea what was going on, but he seemed to be startled when he spotted her.

"Oh, what time is it?" he asked, not bothering to look at the expensive watch he wore on his wrist.

"Amp, you were supposed to pick Jada up over an hour ago. It's nearly nine-thirty and I told you to come get her no later than eight," she said, still holding on to Jada's hand. "Are you moving or something? What is this?"

Without answering, Amp signaled for his daughter to come to him. Paige immediately turned around and headed home, not bothering to repeat her question because there was no mistaking the look she'd seen in his eyes. The man was definitely going through something and she wasn't foolish enough to question him about it. She went inside her home and stood in an upstairs window and watched as they turned off the lights inside the house, closed the back of the moving van, then drove off into darkness.

CHAPTER 23

Sunday evening, Rashad and Melissa finally managed to get together as they had been trying to do the entire weekend. She picked him up on 28th Street in front of his apartment complex, and as part of her little game, she decided that she had to be nice to him if she hoped to attain the information she sought. They had spent nearly two hours tangled up in bumper-to-bumper traffic on the Las Vegas Strip before turning into the parking lot of the Circus Circus Hotel. Her plan was to spend the evening enjoying a nice conversation at the casino's carousel bar, hoping the alcohol would loosen him up so she could find out what he knew about her father's murder.

After stepping onto the slow-moving rotating bar, Rashad and Melissa ordered their drinks before cozying up at a table beside each other. She slowly turned toward him with passion in her eyes and placed her hand on his knee before whispering to him, "I have been thinking about you so much lately. I miss you," she said before sipping her soda.

"I miss you too, and I still can't figure out why you broke up with me."

"Who said I broke up with you?" she asked, acting surprised. "I just needed some time to get my mind together. I had so much going on in my life at the time."

"What was so hard about telling me that?" he asked as he turned to her. "You could have said that you needed some space and I would have been more than happy to give you that. You didn't have to leave me hanging the way you did."

"You're right, Rashad. I apologize."

"Damn, I didn't know what to think. You stopped calling, you stopped returning my calls so I left it alone waiting to see what would happen."

Melissa licked her lips as she slid closer, "I'm sorry, Rashad. God knows I didn't mean to hurt you—I just had more on my plate than I knew how to handle. Is there anything that I can do to make it up to you?"

"Let me think about it," he said with a half-smile.

Leaning forward to kiss his lips, Melissa slipped her tongue inside his mouth and slowly twirled it around his before replying, "Does that help? Do you forgive me now?"

"It's a good start," he said as he leaned in to kiss her again. "Baby, you know that I can't stay mad at you. I care for you too much to stay mad at you."

"Who else have you been kissing, Rashad?" she asked jokingly.

"Nobody. I haven't been with anybody since the last time we were together. You're all I've been able to think about."

"How much do you miss me, Rashad?" she asked while rubbing his chest.

"I miss you a lot, baby."

"Is it me you miss, or do you just miss getting this pussy?"

"That's a good question," he said sarcastically. "Nah, I'm just joking. I miss you. Well, actually, I miss both."

"You might get some tonight if you act right. I miss feeling you between my legs—invading my space."

"I miss it, too. A lot," he replied.

"I want you to fuck me like you did on your birthday. You put something on me thick that night, but you haven't hit this pussy the same since."

"I can fix that," he said, feeling slightly embarrassed. "When we do it again, it'll be better than it was on my birthday."

"Are you being honest with me, Rashad, or is that the alcohol talking?"

"Baby, I have never lied to you about anything. I mean, I do feel a slight buzz coming on, but I wouldn't lie to you about something like that. I miss you for real."

"I want you to give me a baby, Rashad," she whispered. "I think you're everything I've always wanted in a man and I think that you would make a terrific dad. Do you think you would like being my baby's daddy?"

"Of course."

"What about my husband?"

"That too. I've actually thought about it a few times. It was before you cut me off, but I can still see myself being married to you."

"My ideal husband would probably be a lot like my dad was. A man who would take good care of his family and would always know what to do in any situation. I need a good, strong, intelligent man. Do you think you would be able to live up to that?"

"I think so," he nodded.

"That's messed up what your brother did to my dad. He know he didn't have to take it that far."

Suddenly alarmed, Rashad frowned before swallowing the rest of his drink then pulled away from Melissa before replying, "Baby, my brother didn't do anything to your dad. We was at home when that shit went down."

"It's okay, Rashad. You don't have to keep lying for him."

"I'm not lying. My brother was at home with me when your dad was killed. We both saw it on the news the day it happened," he said, clearly agitated. "I don't know who did that shit but I know for sure it wasn't my brother."

"Rashad, I am so tired of you sitting here lying to me," she said while rolling her eyes. "Come on, let me take you home. I'm sick of this bullshit."

She reached into her purse to leave the waiter a tip—secretly pressing the stop button on the recording device that was barely visible under the dim lighting. Once they walked through the casino and entered the parking lot, they climbed inside the Range Rover and didn't say a word to each other as they headed toward the east side of town.

When they pulled up in front of the apartment complex, Melissa fought hard to control her emotions when Rashad hopped out the truck with-out saying good-bye. Melissa was hurt when she sped off. Not because of anything Rashad had done, but more so with herself because she'd failed to get the information she hoped to get.

CHAPTER 24

Three months after being released from jail, Paige Goldwyn was still deeply involved in her secret relationship with Detective Bruno. They spent the entire weekend together in Laughlin, Nevada, a small town near the California border, located 95 miles outside of Las Vegas.

The room had a thick odor in the air that smelled of sex as they lay across the bed—both exhausted. This would be their last evening together before going back home and they really wanted to make the best of it. As they lay in bed in total bliss, Paige rested her head against the detective's shoulder, her hand gently caressing the inside of his thigh, "You're the best, Frank. I never thought I would find a man who would know how to please me the way James did."

It may have been said as a compliment but he was really offended by her remark, "I don't think that this is an appropriate time to be comparing me to him. Why are you even thinking about him?"

"I always think about him," she uttered. "He would probably roll over in his grave if he knew that I had a racist lying in bed with me."

"Please, sweetheart, not this again. Every time you bring this up, we end up arguing until one of us splits."

"That's why they say the truth hurts," she said, wishing she had never started the argument. "Honey, if I didn't care anything about you, I wouldn't be messing around with you the way I do. I just think you need to face reality, because the sooner you do, the sooner we'll be able to resolve your problem."

Uncertain about what she meant, Detective Bruno took a deep breath and blew it out before offering a reply, "And what problem would that be?"

"You're a racist, Frank! If I'm to ever tell my daughters about us, we need to first address your problem and find a solution before I could ever feel comfortable introducing you to them."

"Why do you keep saying I have a problem? I've told you already that I would never do anything to disrespect them and I would never do anything to hurt you intentionally."

"Frank, their dad is the only man they've ever seen me with. I wouldn't ever want to put in their minds that I'm trying to replace him in any way," she explained as her eyes watered. "He could never be replaced and I wouldn't want them to think that I've forgotten about him. I would never do that and I wouldn't want them to forget him either."

"Then why'd you get rid of everything he owned?" he asked boldly. "You've either sold or given away all memorabilia of him, yet you keep bringing up his name like you want him remembered. Besides your daughters, there's nothing left to show that he ever existed. Do you suffer from bipolar disorder, or are you being dishonest when you say these things?"

Jerking away from him, Paige couldn't believe what he'd said to her, "I beg your pardon? I want to remember everything about my husband, and I'll always love him no matter what!"

He clapped his hands and laughed at her, "Oh, now you still love him?"

"Why wouldn't I?"

"Paige, do you really expect me to believe that?"

"Why wouldn't you? Does your racist views block you from seeing it?"

"If your husband does roll over in his grave as you stated earlier, it wouldn't be because I'm a racist, Paige, it would be because he knows you put him there!"

Dumbfounded, she sat up in bed and stared at him, "What? Why would you say something like that to me?"

"If it wasn't for me being what you call a racist, you know your ass would still be in jail right now!"

Confused, Paige's hand quickly covered her mouth as she appeared to be in shock as she turned away, "Why are you saying these things?"

"It's okay, sweetheart. I know what happened," he said in a softer voice. "That's why it was so important for you to go to trial and be acquitted of these allegations. Thanks to the double-jeopardy clause, no matter what you say from this point on, you can never be tried for this again," he said as he pulled her closer to him. "Remember when I first came to the jail to visit you, didn't I tell you that I was in charge of this investigation?"

"Yes," she whispered.

"Before I came down there, I had already made up my mind that I wouldn't let you fall because a nigger had died. That's one less nigger we have to worry about and, to me, that makes the world a better place. Now, on the other hand, if it had been you who'd gotten killed, I would have had every nigger in the city locked up until we got to the bottom of it."

"How'd you know?" she asked delicately.

"The day we did our investigation, we found two bloody fingerprints that came back a match when we compared them to yours. One was taken from the handle of the patio door and the other was found on the back of the showerhead. You never said that you had taken a shower before calling 911."

Showing no signs of remorse, she knew there was no reason to keep pretending, "God, I didn't think I had made any mistakes."

"I knew all of this when I first went to the jail to visit you. I still chose to put my career on the line, because I knew it would be well-worth the risk if I could find a way to save you."

"Does anyone else know?"

"Sweetheart, most of us know. Almost every police officer who was there that day. That's why we all corroborated each other's testimony when we said it was possible that somebody else could have broken in through the patio and committed the crime," he continued. "We all perjured ourselves intentionally to assure one another that we could all be certain no one would talk."

"The code of silence?" she asked.

"You can call it that," he answered bluntly. "What happens in the department stays in the department."

"Then why are you telling me?" she asked with a grin.

"Because I love you, and I know you won't say anything," he said as he wrapped his arm around her. "I wanted to pin this shit on your neighbors, but since they had the means, I couldn't take a chance on them hiring lawyers who could have possibly made it come back to bite me in the ass."

"I'm glad you changed your mind about that. Did you change your mind, or did Bull's murder stop you from pursuing them?"

"Oh no, I knew I wouldn't arrest them for murder long before Bull was killed, but it didn't stop me from harassing their asses every chance I got. Even after Bull got killed, I had one of my guys putting constant pressure on Anthony—going to his house, showing up at his business, threatening he and his family's well-being, acting as if we wanted to extort him, but all we really wanted to do was make him leave. I guess it worked, huh?" he said, laughing.

"Oh, that's why he left so mysteriously. He was acting so weird the last time I saw him. I hope that he and his daughter are doing fine," said Paige. "What happened to the bloody fingerprints you say you found?"

"Everything that could have possibly hurt you at trial was destroyed. I didn't allow the gunpowder residue test to be performed on you because I already knew what the results would be. I couldn't have you ending up at the women's prison on Smiley Road, but I already knew that wouldn't happen."

"How did you get away with all of this?"

"Well, I'm well-connected sweetheart, and I had to call in a few favors. We got some good ol' boys in some very high places so I knew we wouldn't have any serious problems. You know what else?"

"What's that?"

"We gave your lawyer a roadmap on how to defend you. We found out the DA's strategy and fed your attorney the information so he would know how to counter whatever Burch said."

"My lawyer was in on it, too?"

"He was but he didn't know it. That nigger was like a puppet on a string. He fell for everything we put out there for him—we fed him the info through his investigators. We had the judge in our pocket also."

"You had everything all planned out, didn't you?" she asked while kissing his hand.

"Sweetheart, I started planning the moment I laid eyes on you," he replied. "Whatever happened to the weapon we couldn't recover?"

Smiling from ear to ear, she thought for a moment before replying, "What happens in Vegas stays in Vegas, right?"

"I see you're a quick learner. We'll have to discuss it later so we can bring this case to a close once and for all."

"I didn't mean for any of it to happen," she said suddenly. "I just couldn't put up with it anymore. To see him parading around with that other woman. He did it right in front of me like I wasn't even there."

"It's okay, babe," he whispered. "It was definitely his loss. What man in his right mind would mess around when he's got a woman like you at home? Whoever she was, how could she have possibly compared to you?"

"I don't know. I was never interested in getting to know her," Paige said as she turned to him. "She's the tall redheaded receptionist who works with my daughters. She would always come in faking like she wanted to get breast implants, but all she was really trying to do was spend time with him. It happened nearly every day. They would always laugh and talk while she took all these pictures. I think they were intentionally trying to torment me."

"You'd had enough?"

Paige gave Detective Bruno a look that immediately provided an answer for him, "I'd had more than enough! As soon as he and that kid began arguing, I knew it would be the perfect opportunity to pull it off."

"Your instincts were right, and you don't have to worry about it no more. Sweetheart, it's over and done with and it's time for you to move on with your life," he said in a caring voice. "Your husband got what he had coming to him. To me, black is black. Whether he was a doctor, lawyer, or whatever. He was still a nigger!"

Six months later, while Detective Frank Bruno was still the lead detective in the case, Marcus Myers was tried and convicted for the first-degree murder of James Goldwyn. It appears that after being pulled over for allegedly running a red-light, his vehicle was searched and an unregistered firearm was found in the glove compartment. Once he was taken into custody for possessing the weapon, a ballistics report later revealed that the gun had been used in the unsolved murder of Dr. James Goldwyn.

www.ingramcontent.com/pod-product-compliance
Lightning Source LLC
Chambersburg PA
CBHW022109170626
46808CB00002B/662